the NOBODIES

ALSO BY N. E. BODE

THE ANYBODIES

the NOBODIES
by N. E. BODE

Illustrated by PETER FERGUSON

HARPERCOLLINSPUBLISHERS

Library of Congress Cataloging-in-Publication Data

Bode, N. E.

The Nobodies / by N. E. Bode ; illustrated by Peter Ferguson.— 1st ed.

p.   cm.

Summary: Now reunited with her real family, eleven-year-old Fern
goes to a camp to learn to practice the Anybody magic, where she
unexpectedly faces the evil Mole, who has imprisoned the mysterious
Nobodies in his factory basement.

ISBN 0-06-055738-9 — ISBN 0-06-055739-7 (lib. bdg.)

[1. Magic—Fiction.   2. Camps—Fiction.   3. Books and reading—
Fiction.   4. Brothers and sisters—Fiction.   5. Love—Fiction.
6. Characters in literature—Fiction.]   I. Ferguson, Peter, 1968– ill.
II. Title.

PZ7.B63362 2005   2004021501

[Fic]—dc22   CIP

AC

Typography by Karin Paprocki

1 2 3 4 5 6 7 8 9 10

❖

First Edition

THIS BOOK IS DEDICATED
to Nobodies everywhere in every
shape and form. Aren't we all
Nobodies in one way or another?
I know I am.

ACKNOWLEDGMENTS

I DON'T DO ALL THIS ALONE, YOU KNOW. I RELY on trusty folks who read my work early on in the process and write things in the margins like: Swell! Stinky! Do-over! Go forth! And I want to thank them for all their reading and jotting—my editor, Alix Reid, who is so brilliant she sometimes glows—just lights up from within; and my favorite people to be with, day in and day out: David G. W. Scott, Phoebe, Finneas, and Theo. I'd like to express my adoration of Molly Baggott—always inspiring—and Lola the Great, and all of the readers who've dropped me fantastic e-mails—especially Alex, Stephanie, and Sammy.

There's a bunch of folks who wear suits and occasionally go to fancy lunches on my behalf—Nat Sobel (essential), Justin Manask (my go-to), and Joel Gotler (of precious face-time). I want to thank the indomitable Clare Anne Conlon and all of her wonderful peeps, plus Amy Burton, Lauren Velevis, and Maggie McMahon.

I'd like to thank Julianna Baggott, who, frankly, was a little more help with the first book, but in the end turns out to be completely necessary to my creative process.

And, of course, I'd like to thank Nobodies of every kind—not just those described in this book. My pages are always open to you.

Prologue   1

PART 1
The Start of All the Trouble

1 Diet Lime Fizzy Drinks   13
2 Charge!   31
3 Good Old Bixie   41
4 The Storm   49
5 To Whom It May Concern 60

PART 2
Camp Happy Sunshine
Good Times

1 Blind as a . . . *Bus Driver*? 71
2 The Hermit Warning   81
3 And . . . Mole Holes   94
4 Mary Stern Gets
   What's Coming to Her   102
5 The Bonfire   115

PART 3
Night Creatures

1 The New Rule   131
2 Kicked Out   138

3   Nurse Hurley   149
4   Claussen Peevish—
    Stricken!   159
5   Cancellation, Memorization
    and Assimilation   166

PART 4
Wanted: Fern!

1   Into the Woods   181
2   The Breathing Trees   189
3   The Hermitage   203
4   The Search Party   225
5   Holmquist and His
    Mommy   234

PART 5
The Factory Basement

1   Basements, Basements
    Everywhere   249
2   The Nobodies   264
3   Springing a Leak   272
4   On the Avenue of the
    Americas   278
5   And . . .
    Wait! There's More!   288

PROLOGUE

I am writing this second book while truly *terrified*.

The problem is the pressing issue of my old writing teacher! I once thought he was the greatest writing teacher on earth, but, as it turns out, he is more than a little crazy. Since the publication of Book One, *The Anybodies*, he has made it known that I am his sworn enemy.

At first it was a literary feud, which means that we mostly wrote mean things about each other. (I confess the words "dimwit" and "windbag" were both used.) Literary feuds usually end there. You rarely see even a nasty pinch or slap fight if two feuding authors meet up, face-to-face, at some bookish function. *But*, I tell you, this man has lost his marbles, and I know that he's watching my every move and wants to do me grave harm.

You see, this whole story (Books One and Two) was told to me on a broken-down subway car. I was N. E. Bode then, just as I am now, but nobody knew it because I hadn't yet published my first book. I was younger and, I think, sweeter then, a little pie-eyed and dopey. It was the beginning of the school year, and I admit I was the type of student who walked around like I'd been thunked on the head with a blunt object. I was either so shocked by what I'd just learned or so terribly bored that I'd gone into a stupor. Either way I had this dumbstruck expression that was pretty unreadable.

This time, walking onto the subway car, I was dumbstruck in an excited, jangly way. My writing teacher—the one mentioned above—had told the entire class that they were in the presence of the most dim-witted student this teacher had ever come across in all his illustrious days, and that this specific type of dim-wittery could be the future demise of literature. I was looking around, craning my neck to see just which one of us, exactly, when he said, "Ladies and gentlemen, N. E. Bode."

Now, an hour or so later, I was still a little flushed by it all. I was pretty excited that he knew my name at all. (How simple I was then! How dimpled with innocence!)

I barely noticed that I had sat down next to a young girl of about ten or eleven. She was ordinary looking except for her overly large eyes and this odd flop of curly hair that stood up on her head quite roosterlike. She seemed nervous. She was holding a stack of books—two small diaries with locks and one fat volume. All around the girl there were sopping wet kids near her own age. One of them, a pale, chubby boy, was leaning against her shoulder, snoring loudly. I would come to find out his name was Howard.

Now subways are tricky. They rattle. The lights sometimes flicker, dim, then blip back on. They're always threatening to come to a screeching breakdown. Generally all the flickering and blipping and rattling is just an empty threat. They chug on. But this time the subway actually did come to a grinding halt in the middle of a tunnel. The lights flicked out. The engine went dead. The girl gasped. It was stuffy. Everyone was silent, but electrically so. You know how it is being in the dark with strangers. It's disconcerting . . . like those few moments before the movie comes on the screen and you just feel kind of vulnerable and silly.

I whispered, "I think it's going to be okay, really."

She whispered back, "I'm not so sure. Things aren't always what they seem, you know."

"I didn't know that," I whispered, because at that

point I'd really been taking everything pretty much for what it seemed to be. In fact, I was fairly sure that my type could bring about the demise of literature, just because my writing professor had said so.

And so the girl and I started up a hushed conversation. This was when she started telling me who she was and what she was doing here, and that she had had a nerve-wracking day, fighting an evil mind, and how this had made her a little edgy and nervous about things like broken-down subway cars.

She explained to me everything, half of which, later, with extensive research on my own part, became *The Anybodies*. If you haven't done so, I suggest reading it, even if you zip through it in a speedy speed-reading way with a zigzagging finger and some time spent with the illustrations, which are the work of Mr. Peter Ferguson, an ornery genius. It isn't necessary, though. In fact, here, let me get to the main terms of that first book.

1. AN ANYBODY—a person who by nature or training (concentration and sometimes hypnosis) can transform objects into reality (for example, there once was a girl who reached into a painting of a fishpond to pet the fish) and who can transform themselves into other shapes (a nun into a lamppost, a bad guy into a bull). Anybodies are shape changers, in a way, but, as you'll see, there's more to it explained in this book.

2. FERN—this is the name of the girl mentioned in the definition above. An unusual girl who finds out that she is, indeed, an Anybody from a long line of Anybodies.

3. THE BONE—Fern's father. He was a washed-up Anybody who was not naturally gifted, and he now lives with Fern and Fern's grandmother in her grandmother's boardinghouse.

4. ELIZA—Fern's mother. She was a great Anybody. She died in childbirth, but Fern still feels her mother's presence.

5. HOWARD—a boy, Fern's age. Howard was supposed to belong to the Drudgers—a pair of tragically dull accountants—and Fern was supposed to belong to the world of the Anybodies. But they were swapped at birth and not unswapped until the beginning of the 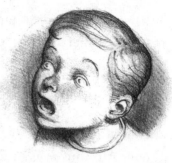 summer when Fern and Howard were eleven years old.

6. *THE ART OF BEING ANYBODY* **BY OGLETHORP HENCEFORTHTOWITH**—a one-of-a-kind book that holds all the secrets of being an Anybody and can only be read by the person who the book belongs to. And the book now belongs to Fern.

7. **THE MISER**—an ex–bad guy, a reformed villain, who was friends with Fern's father when they were boys, then, consumed with jealousy, hated him and landed the Bone in jail. In *The Anybodies* he sought revenge.

But he's now friends with Fern's father again and is also staying at Fern's grandmother's boardinghouse.

8. FERN'S GRANDMOTHER'S BOARDINGHOUSE—

a house that exists in a world of books. It's even constructed with books as the main building supply! The house is populated with creatures that have been shaken from books—Borrowers in the walls, hobbits in the yard, Indians in the cupboards. It's situated where the sidewalk ends, beside a peach tree with the most enormous, one might say *giant* peach.

9. THE GREAT REALDO—the greatest of all Anybodies, the Great Realdo is a force for good, and is, in

fact, Fern's grandmother, Dorathea Gretel.

Good enough? Does that help?

Okay then, let's get back up to speed!

Fern went on to tell me how she and Howard came to be in the city, surrounded by a pack of sleeping kids. And who could have known that Fern and I would form an alliance, a promise, and set things right? Who could have known?

The subway started up. The lights flickered on. Fern came to her stop. She and the kids got out. She waved to me from the platform. I waved back.

And so, while I'm dodging attempts on my life (Is it just a coincidence that I was almost hit by a bus? Is it just a coincidence that the tea I accidentally spilled in a restaurant—before sipping it—hissed and foamed, disintegrating the tabletop? The broken ladder . . . the elevator that plunged—quite empty—to the pit of my dentist's office building just as I stepped off? Coincidences? I think not!), I will also be writing this book and keeping my sworn oath, my promise, made to Fern that hot afternoon.

Hopefully I will remain in one piece so that I can get to the end and tell this true story once and for all.

Sincerely (and I mean that!),

N E Bode

DIET LIME FIZZY DRINKS

FERN WAS LOOKING OUT HER BEDROOM WINDOW in her grandmother's house for a runaway rhinoceros. Ridiculous, you might be muttering to yourself. Well, it might be ridiculous, but it's true. (And didn't your mother tell you not to mutter to yourself! My mother told me that if I muttered to myself all the time, I might end up spending my days shuffling through the bus depot wearing my pajamas. And so I've made a little life out of muttering on paper—just like so.)

Fern had been sent to her bedroom by Dorathea and the Bone, who were steamed about the rhinoceros that Howard and Fern had accidentally shaken from a book containing an entire stampede. They'd been shaking the book together, but once Fern heard the stampede pounding in the book, she had dropped it. She'd told Howard to shut it, quick, but he hadn't. Howard! Fern could see him now in her mind's eye, gripping onto the roaring, thundering book, his whole body rattling while the rhino muscled its way out, bursting forth with its horn and thick armored sides! Why hadn't he listened to her? Howard, with his love of spray starch and ironing boards and wristwatches, was the most boring kid she knew. *Well,* Fern thought, *he sure picked a fine time to be drawn to excitement!*

Howard had been sent to his bedroom too, which was wedged up in the attic. Fern hoped that he was feeling miserable up there and very hot.

Really, all Fern wanted now was to go to camp— which would happen tomorrow. Camp Happy Sunshine Good Times was a camp for young Anybodies. It wasn't called Camp Anybody, because Anybodies don't want to be known. So it disguised itself in the sappy brochures as an inspirational camp built on the sentimental notions of hand-holding, sing-alongs and crafts where campers color in pictures of kids in baseball caps under the caption "I am so special!" It weeded out the non-Anybodies by a questionnaire and, if in person, by a wink. (You see, if an Anybody winks at another Anybody, they have to wink back. It's unavoidable.) At camp Fern was sure she'd find kids more like her—not like Howard, a clumsy Anybody hugging his math books, Howard, who was always dull except when he *should* be dull!

The Drudgers had dropped Howard off the week before camp, an entire week ahead of schedule. Why? Fern had wondered. The Drudgers said it was so that Fern and Howard could spend time together before camp. But Fern now thought that the Drudgers were a little afraid of Howard. (He'd hypnotized them into monkeys for the first half of the summer, all to impress his new friend, Milton Beige, and when Fern saw the Drudgers as they dropped Howard off, she noticed that they still had some leftover monkey tendencies—eyeing the treetops and occasionally flaring their nostrils.) Fern didn't blame the Drudgers for dumping Howard earlier than planned. She wished she could dump him right back.

Fern had been trying to ignore Howard as best as she could, but it wasn't easy. Ever since Howard first showed up at Fern's grandmother's house, he walked around like a sad dog, kicked out of the house for chewing the carpet. He missed the Drudgers and especially Milton Beige, whom he called on the phone daily to talk about math equations and his dread of the upcoming camp. (Fern sometimes eavesdropped on these conversations. She could tell that even Milton Beige—who was supposed to be extremely dull—was actually more interested in talking about Fern's grandmother's house and Anybody camp and Anybody business in general than Howard was.) When not on the phone with Milton, Howard was complaining. He didn't like Fern's grandmother's house—its strange landscape dotted with chimneys, the big house roofed with books. He complained about the books, books, books . . . everywhere!

"The house is crammed nearly solid!" Howard whined. "Who can breathe with all this dust?"

It was true. Dusty books lined every wall and were fitted into every small space—cupboards, drawers, knee-holes of desks. They were sewn into the stuffing of the sofa cushions, even crammed into the paintings hung on the wall—a little trick that Fern's mother had invented when she was a girl about Fern's age. To get around in the house, everyone was forced to careen along narrow, book-lined paths. Fern loved this! Each book contained worlds and adventures. Sometimes she could feel the energy of the books radiating out from them.

Howard, however, was simply annoyed.

Howard didn't like the creatures who lived on the premises either. He shooed the hobbits in the yard. He scolded the Borrowers for stealing his toothbrush and buttons. And he shushed the crows when they started fighting—loudly and with great conviction—about the best places to find bloated worms. Fern went around apologizing to the creatures for Howard's grumpiness.

And he certainly didn't enjoy living with the Miser, who used to be quite evil but now wore a soft, meek expression. Here Fern couldn't really blame Howard. He'd grown up in fear of the Miser, and no matter how many times Fern told Howard that the Miser had changed, Howard couldn't quite believe it. Fern had to forgive this, because of Howard's past associations with the Miser.

But she couldn't forgive the fact that Howard thought Fern's grandmother, Dorathea, was a nut, even though this was a bit true. Fern made him help her read to Dorathea at night. Dorathea liked to read as many books as possible, all at the same time, a sentence from one book, then the next, then the next. With Howard and Fern, she could juggle six stories at once.

"Impossible!" Howard would say later on. "She can't possibly keep them all straight! She's just showing off! What's wrong with reading one book at a time? Like normal people!"

Now this afternoon leading up to the rhino incident, the last day before camp, Fern had gotten tired of ignoring Howard and his complaints. The loneliness was gnawing at her. She walked into the living room, where Howard had sprawled out with his math book. She begged him to get his nose out of the book. "Come out to the garden, please! I'll bring *The Art of Being Anybody*, and you can try to shake things from books again. I'll help you this time. I promise!" They'd worked in the garden together before. Howard wasn't very good at being an Anybody. He'd once shaken a book on the ocean for a whole hour and only got three drops of sea-water to drip out.

Howard was ignoring her as best he could, and then his head snapped up. He had an idea. He said, "I'm only going *if* you promise to shake my math book."

"Your math book?" Fern said. "What could possibly pop out of a math book?"

"What if numbers fall out? Or equations? Or concepts?"

"Who would want to see those things?" Fern said.

Howard thought a minute. "Or," he said, "maybe a train might try to nudge its way out of the book, a train from one of those word problems—if a train arrives at two forty-five in Circleville, which is forty-three miles from—"

"A train?" Those word problems frustrated Fern beyond belief, but she liked the idea of a train.

"It's just an idea," said Howard. "I mean, you're not allowed to really shake a train. Remember the lizard!"

"I know, I know," Fern said. She'd already gotten in a little trouble earlier that summer because of an angry lizard that she'd mistakenly shaken from a book. The lizard had bitten most everyone now. And so she was only allowed to shake out less dangerous things like a grapefruit spoon, a brandy snifter, a gravy ladle. "We'll be careful. Bring it."

They'd walked downstairs and through the kitchen, where Dorathea was canning peaches. She'd been canning peaches for weeks, it seemed. The giant peach from the tree in the backyard had finally gotten ripe. Fern's grandmother had whipped up peach jam, peach muffins, peach soup, peach potatoes, peach porridge, peach burgers and the vaguely sinister peach surprise. Still, there was so much peach left over that the canned peaches were fighting the books for space in the basement. Even the Borrowers who lived in the house had complained about only having peach-tainted food items to steal. The peachy smell of the kitchen made Fern a little queasy. She wanted to pinch her nose, but didn't because it might insult her grandmother.

"Hello, kiddos!" Dorathea said. "Nearly ready for camp?"

"No," Howard said grumpily.

"Yes!" said Fern, thinking how it would free her from

grumpy Howard. You have to keep in mind that Fern had felt different all of her life, and she was desperate to meet folks more like her—Anybodies. At camp she would be normal, for once.

They slipped out the back door.

The Bone and the Miser were concentrating on the giant peach pit, which, they were thinking, could be sawed in half, dug out and made into two sizeable boats. The Bone was wearing jeans and a work shirt. He had a book about mighty ships under his arm. He'd really taken to reading. Hard not to in a house filled with books—well, *made* of books. He'd changed a good bit too. When Howard had arrived, the Bone walked up to him and wrapped his arms around him, lifting him off the ground slightly. This surprised Howard, because he wasn't used to the Bone being so free and loose with his affection. The Bone had raised Howard with his emotions in check, for fear of loving someone too much only to lose them. It had taken him a long time to feel whole again after the death of his wife, Eliza (Fern's mother, remember? If not, refer to page 5) just after Fern was born.

"Hey!" called the Bone. "We're thinking of giant sails! Real craftsmanship! What do you say?"

"Sounds a little dangerous," said Howard.

"Sounds great!" said Fern.

"Well," the Miser said, "we may never sail them. I'd be happy just to have them stay right here, dry-docked."

"No, no," the Bone said. "If I've said it once, I've said it a million times—we're going to have adventures again, Miser! You can't hide here all your life!"

The Miser nodded. "I know, I know," he said, but his expression disagreed. His expression seemed to be saying, *Yes, we can. We can hide right here for the rest of our lives.* The misadventures that the Miser had had as an evildoer had really scared him. There was nothing miserly about the Miser anymore. He was no longer shaggy. His white beard and his large floating eyebrows had disappeared, revealing a sweet, flushed face. But he was still scared of himself, in a way, and scared in general, too. The Bone was set on breaking him of all that fear, which was one of the reasons for building the peach-pit ships.

"What are you two up to?" the Bone asked, pointing at the books in their arms. "Taking it easy, I hope. Being careful."

"That's right!" said Fern.

"Nothing with legs," the Bone said.

"No teeth," the Miser added anxiously. He'd gotten a nasty bite on his big toe from the lizard.

"I promise!" Fern said, and, at that moment, she truly meant it. In fact, in addition to Howard's math book and *The Art of Being Anybody*, the only other book Fern had brought was a book on housewares. They walked over to the far side of the garden.

Howard was slouched and unhappy. Fern wished that he liked all this more. In fact, Fern wished she could make Howard like being with *her* more. She'd thought of hypnotizing him. She'd even read over Chapter Three of *The Art of Being Anybody* about hypnotizing others. But Oglethorp Henceforthtowith's writing was so hard to understand! It went something like this: "It's best, essentially and critically and politically and judiciously, to look the person in the eye, the way one would an eyeless alien, the kind that might come after your dog in the middle of the night, tunneling up from the dirt." The dog tunneling up? Or was the alien tunneling up, or the night itself? How do you look an eyeless alien in the eye, anyway? The book itself was a hypnotized object. It was readable only by its owner, Fern, and so Fern couldn't even get anyone else to help make sense of it for her.

Fern said, "Look, Howard. Let's start simply. How about you try first to shake out a saltshaker. Just that. From my housewares book. I'm sure you can do it."

Fern meant this as encouragement, but Howard didn't take it that way. He was insulted. "Don't talk down to me, Fern."

This steamed Fern. She was trying to be nice! "You'd like it if you could just feel what it's like!"

"Don't you think I'd like to? Don't you think that it's dawned on me that it must be pretty great to shake something from a book?" Howard was pouty, squinting in the bright sun.

"Here," Fern said, demonstrating. "I think of a saltshaker. I turn to a page on saltshakers. I shake and think and shake and think. It's easy. It's simple."

And here's where things started to go wrong. Fern was holding the book wide open, shaking firmly but

gently, but instead of a saltshaker, a green bottle
plopped out of the book. A bottle
of Diet Lime Fizzy Drink.

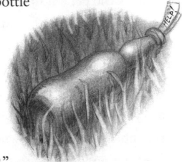

Howard laughed. He'd
never had the opportunity to
laugh at Fern before. She'd
always been perfect. "What's
that? Are you sure you weren't
thinking about being thirsty?"

"No," Fern said. "I wasn't." She didn't even pick up
the bottle. She started again, thinking of a saltshaker
and shaking. But again a bottle of Diet Lime Fizzy Drink
plopped out. It was green, and a bit dusty, uncapped,
already guzzled.

Howard picked up one of the bottles. "Huh," he
said.

Fern was shaking again, more vigorously this time
on a different page, and three more bottles plopped to
the ground. She quickly turned the page to place set-
tings. She thought of spoons, then forks, then scented
candles, but only got Diet Lime Fizzy Drinks.

"Wait," Howard said. "Just wait. Look." He held one
of the bottles up to the light. "There's something in it."

And there was. A rolled-up piece of paper. The
paper was rolled up tightly so that with some shaking
and angling, Howard finally got it to slip out of the

bottle's neck onto the grass.

Fern picked it up and flattened it on her thigh. She read aloud:

"Help us! Trust no one, especially grown-ups. We need you!"

"They need me?" Fern said.

"Or maybe they need *me*! If I'd read it, it could have been me!" Howard said.

This was true, Fern realized. Now she and Howard started racing to pick up bottles and wheedle the notes out as fast as they could.

Howard read: *He is after you. Watch out.*

"Who's he?" Howard asked, reaching for another bottle.

Fern read: *Beware. Save us.*

"But who are you?" Fern asked.

Howard read: *Are you listening?*

"Yes," he said, "we are!"

Fern read: *It's awful. We need you!*

"Yes, yes!" Fern said impatiently. "We get it!"

Howard read: *He's terrible. He's sinister. How will we survive?*

"I don't know," Howard answered.

And then Fern read this note: *Fern, we know you have the powers to defeat him. Please find us!*

And Howard read his next note in a defeated voice: *We don't know where we are. It is awful, dark. Are you there, Fern?*

So they *did* mean Fern! This shocked her. It was so inexplicable, so odd to have these strangers suddenly call her by name that it made her stomach do a flip-flop. She was the one they wanted to help her. Not just anyone. Not Howard. She was here, listening, but she wasn't sure who she was listening to and what exactly they were trying to tell her.

"They aren't giving a lot of information," Howard

said. "How do they expect you to help? And why you? Why not me? I could help, you know. I'm standing right here too. I can be helpful!"

"How do they know my name?" Fern asked, staring at the bottles and notes now littering the ground around their feet. "How do you think they know about me?"

"Well, they've heard about your battle with the Miser, that's obvious," Howard said with a hint of jealousy.

"But no one knows about that. At least, no one outside the family. My grandmother didn't want news to get out among the Anybodies. She said it would change my life too much. I wasn't ready for it." Fern was still a little disappointed about this. She wanted to be famous, of course. Who doesn't? (I do. I want people to stop me in restaurants and ask me to sign their dinner napkins.)

Howard walked around in a little circle. He scratched his head. He said, "Well, what happens if we both try to shake a book? Would we still get a bottle?"

Fern looked at Howard. This was the first time he'd ever suggested that they try something together. It made Fern happy inside, although she didn't show it.

"If you hold one side of the book and I hold the other," Howard said, "then at least I'll know what it feels like." He picked up his math book.

It wasn't his fault that he stunk at being an Anybody,

27

and it wasn't her fault that she was good at it. Maybe if they worked together? Why hadn't Fern thought of it? He turned to a page of word problems.

"Okay," Fern said.

They held the book up and shook. But it's hard to shake a book in unison—it takes practice to do things in unison. I was on a synchronized swimming team while at the Axim School for the Remarkably Giftless, and I tell you it was challenging, especially since none of us could swim. We'd flop, gag and yell at one another. In any case, I'm sorry to report that on page 147 of Howard's math book, there was a word problem about, you guessed it, a stampede of rhinoceros. As soon as Fern felt the book grow heavy, very heavy, she let go, remembering her promise to stick to housewares.

"Close it, Howard," she shouted over the growing racket of distant hooves echoing from the book. "Close it!"

But Howard was too excited. This was the closest he'd ever come, and there was one inch inside of Howard that actually loved the idea of excitement. (Let's remember he *did* hypnotize the Drudgers into thinking they were monkeys.) His body rumbling and vibrating, he reached for the side that Fern had dropped and jerked it upright. A giant horn appeared first, quickly followed by a rhinoceros's big head with its wide eyes. Howard's cheeks flushed and jiggled as he tried to steady his legs.

Fern stumbled backward. "No, Howard!"

Now the rhino's bulky shoulders forced the book to stretch and bend. Its hooves hit the ground, followed by its armored back, its wide ribs and haunches. Its final shove out of the book knocked Howard and the book to the ground. Finally all that could be seen was its nearly hairless tail as it galloped off.

Now being this close to a large horned animal is terrifying. I happen to know firsthand, because just recently I was attacked by an angry bull while sitting in a field of daisies, trying to write the beginning of this very chapter. The bull had a nose ring, like the girl who works at my favorite coffee shop. But unlike the girl with the nose ring, who's simply a little jittery from caffeine, the bull was ferociously angry. He charged me, and I barely had time to scamper up the bows of a pine tree. I don't scamper well, and I almost perished. (Was this the work of my insane writing professor, you ask? Well, it's impossible to prove, but I have my theories. . . .) I suppose it's better at least to have the giant horned animal running *away* from you than *at* you, but Fern and Howard were both very shaken—and Howard was literally shaken.

"Howard!" Fern said angrily. "Now you've done it."

She collected the notes from the bottles that were scattered on the ground. "I warned you. . . ." She was mad at herself, too. She'd be in trouble, and there would be no real way of explaining a rhinoceros, which not only had legs but teeth and a horn. And more so, she was sad that Howard's idea of doing something together, something almost the way a brother and sister might, had gone so badly.

Howard looked up at her through a cloud of dust, utterly dazed. He picked up the bottles, cradling them in his arms.

"C'mon!" Fern said angrily "Let's go tell on ourselves."

"What?" Howard uttered. "Why?"

"I think that it might be worse if my grandmother and father happen to just run into a rhinoceros. Harder to explain then, don't you think?"

Howard nodded reluctantly. They both looked off into the distance and watched the rhinoceros's white horn disappear into a field of tall corn.

CHARGE!

FERN AND HOWARD FOUND THE BONE AND THE
Miser sawing the giant peach pit—a wheezing racket.
As the kids walked up, the Bone smiled, and they both
stopped sawing. There was a sudden silence. The two
men were covered in bits of pit. And then the Bone
took in the two kids' glum faces, and his expression
changed. Suddenly worried, he asked them what was
wrong.

Fern told them about the rhino as quickly as she
could in a nervous sputter of information, and Howard
stood beside her nodding along.

The Miser was obviously frightened. "What a bad

idea!" he muttered. "A bad, bad idea!" He glanced around nervously.

The Bone was angry, but he wasn't very good at being angry. He didn't have much practice at being angry. His cheeks went red, though, and his brow furrowed. Fern felt awful. Howard was shifting his weight beside her. The Bone said, "Well, I'm not sure I know much about the habits of rhinos. The Miser and I will keep an eye out and think. And you two should go inside where it's safe, and"—this is the part that Fern had hoped to skip—"tell your grandmother everything."

Fern dreaded the idea of telling her grandmother. Dorathea didn't like any misuse of being an Anybody. Fern had no idea how she'd react. Although Fern had never seen her angry, she knew that her grandmother was an excitable and powerful woman. Fern was scared.

Howard and Fern trudged across the yard and inside the house. Fern saw her grandmother's back curled over the peach jars on the kitchen table.

"Excuse me," Fern said. "There's a bit of a problem."

"Is there?" her grandmother said, turning around. "Come and sit down."

And so Fern and Howard pulled out two kitchen chairs. Fern looked at Howard. She'd told the Bone, so it was his turn. But Howard just stared back at Fern blankly. "You go," Fern whispered.

"You go," Howard whispered back.

"No, you go!"

"No, you!"

"I'd go," Dorathea said, "but I don't know what this is about."

And so Fern told her the whole story, starting with Howard's math book and ending with the rhino's horn disappearing from sight.

Dorathea listened, folding her peach-stained hands on the table. And when Fern was finished, Dorathea was quiet for a minute. Then she said, "You know this is serious business. This isn't a game. It's not to be messed with for entertainment! Don't you two know the powers involved here?" She glowered at them. Fern, who had been going to mention the notes, now shoved them in her pocket. It didn't seem the time to bring those up. And Howard had thrown out all of the bottles, except one, Fern noticed, which he had hidden under his leg. "Well, maybe you don't fully understand the powers involved here. Maybe that's why you need to go to camp to get a fuller education with Holmquist, the guru!" Fern had heard her grandmother speak highly of Holmquist, the camp director who'd become an Anybody guru since he'd stopped being ruled by "that-mother-of-his," as Dorathea put it.

Dorathea was now shaking her head, looking at Fern.

"I'm surprised at you!"

Fern felt hot and sweaty. She felt like her stomach was curdling. She looked at Howard, and he looked guilty too. Dorathea sent them to their rooms. On the way up the stairs, Howard said, "I'm sorry, Fern. Really! I'll fix it! You'll see."

"You can't fix this, Howard. You just can't."

And so now you know why Fern was there, in her bedroom, looking out her window for a rhino. But the awfulness doesn't end there. No, no! We're only on Chapter Two, you know! It would be very dull if things only got better and sweeter and happier from here on out!

Fern heard a clatter, bustling, clomping coming from Howard's attic room. Then she heard what sounded like heavy boots banging down the stairs.

"Howard?" she called out. "Is that you?"

But there was no answer. The boots clomped on. The front door opened and banged shut, and then it was quiet again.

Fern opened her bedroom door a crack and looked up and down the empty hallway. "Howard!" she called. "Howard?"

Then she heard Howard's sneakers on the narrow attic stairs and there was Howard's face, with a tomato's shine and bursting with pride. "I fixed it, Fern. I told you I would and I did. Without any help at all!"

"What?" Fern asked. "How did you fix it, Howard?" She had a very bad feeling about this.

"Well, I got a book out and I shook and shook and shook."

"What? What were you trying to shake out?"

"A big-game hunter, of course! Who else would fix this situation? You can't call in a regular old exterminator like you've got a bad case of ants!"

Fern didn't say a word. She took off running down the stairs. Howard ran after her. "What's wrong? I fixed it, I told you!"

But Fern was panicked. A big-game hunter? With a gun? She ran out the front door and into the yard, looking over the hobbit chimneys in every possible direction. She'd have to tell Dorathea and the Bone! It would be even worse than the last time! It wasn't her fault, but would they see it that way? Howard was standing beside her, all out of breath.

"It's going to be fine!" he said.

But it was too late for that kind of peppiness. There was a loud clap, like thunder, but it wasn't thunder. The sky was a bright blue.

"It's him!" Howard exclaimed.

And then there was a pounding noise from the other side of the house, and then another enormous crack, a boom, a gunshot.

The pounding grew louder. In the backyard the Miser and the Bone started shouting. Then louder pounding, and all the commotion was in the house now! In the kitchen Dorathea screamed. Books started trembling and falling off the roof onto the ground around Fern and Howard. The front door flew open and two jars of peaches leaped into the air and out the door and shattered on the sidewalk. Fern's grandmother charged behind them, followed by the Bone, holding blueprints of half a giant peach pit, and then, lastly, the Miser. They dove onto Fern and Howard, covering them in a big heap. The hooves grew louder and louder. And then the rhinoceros bounded through the front door, splintering wood on either side with its armor. It tossed its giant horns this way and that, trying to decide which way to go.

There was another gunshot from inside the house. The rhinoceros galloped off toward a distant wood, leaping over hobbit chimneys.

Slowly Dorathea and the Bone and the Miser lifted their heads and looked around. Fern popped her head up. The dust was still thick. Someone coughed and then someone else. And then there was the sound of boots in the doorway. Everyone looked up to see a skinny old man with a bloated belly. He was wearing a pith helmet and puffy knee-buttoned pants which Fern thought were called jodhpurs. He had high kneesocks and a veil

of netting hanging off the front of his helmet, like a confused widow. He looked bewildered and frightened. He said, "Is it gone? I should say, I'm not very good at this. Is it teatime? I'd like some tea. My nerves are rattled." He looked around at the shocked expressions. "I do apologize for barging in."

He looked at his gun with its fluted barrel as if he'd never seen it before. It was a big old elaborate gun, the kind that belongs in a museum. He was fiddling with it nervously, pointing it up into the doorframe. And then, much to his surprise, the gun went off again. He glanced up to the blasted spot in the top of the door-frame and put the gun down by his boots. "Oh, my! I'm sorry. It doesn't do this in the book, you see. It never goes off."

By this point hobbits had wandered up from their underground homes. They clustered now, chatting to one another.

Howard looked at Fern and Fern looked at Howard. Howard seemed ready to cry, but he didn't.

The Miser and the Bone were still dazed. The Bone's blueprint of the peach pit was now ripped, but he didn't notice. He was waiting, like everyone else, for some sort of explanation.

"Fern?" he said. "Howard?"

"I thought I was helping!" Howard said. "I shook

a big-game hunter out of a book so he could hunt the rhino!"

"How?" Fern asked.

"Your powers must have brushed off on me. I don't know." Howard couldn't help it. Despite the big mess and his sadness about the big mess, the charging rhino and the incompetent hunter, he was a little bit proud of himself.

Fern was really angry, though. "This was your great idea about how to get rid of the rhino!"

The Bone and the Miser looked at Howard, completely confused.

Howard nodded, a little ashamed now.

"Where did he come from? What book? We'll have to put him back," the Bone said.

The Miser was ashen with fear. "This is awful! Terrible!"

Dorathea was already standing up, brushing off her skirt. She clapped her hands to get everyone's attention. She was the best Anybody among them. In fact, as you may recall from the glossary of terms in the letter at the beginning of the book, she was the Great Realdo—possibly the greatest Anybody in the world—though few knew it. She said, "Howard must have gotten him from a dictionary. He isn't a real hunter. He's only the general idea of a hunter. Anyone can see that. But he's harmless now that he's put down that gun. Let's go inside."

The nervous big-game hunter, or at least the idea of the big-game hunter, picked burrs off his jodhpurs tenderly. Then he tried to smile, giving a reminder. "Teatime?" he inquired, adding the discreet gesture of raising a cup to his lips, his pinkie curved out just so.

GOOD OLD BIXIE

DICTIONARY VERSIONS OF PEOPLE ARE NEVER AS interesting as real people. The general idea of the big-game hunter wasn't good company, and teatime became pretty tedious.

The Bone suggested that the old gent tell some hunting stories.

The Miser said, "Yes, tell us a story of great adventure."

The big-game hunter just sat there at the kitchen table, peering at everyone through the books stacked thick as underbrush. He smiled politely, cleared his throat a number of times as if just about to launch into something, but then . . . nothing.

"He can't," Fern's grandmother said, passing around a bowl of lemon wedges.

"Why not?" asked the Bone.

The big-game hunter cleared his throat again. "I don't have any outlandish stories to tell about adventure, although I should, shouldn't I?"

Fern and Howard nodded. Yes, they were fairly sure that he should.

"It seems like part of the definition of a big-game hunter, but I've never ridden elephants through jungles or that sort of thing. I only know my spot in the dictionary under 'big-game hunter,' between 'Bigfoot' and 'biggle.'"

"Oh," they all said collectively.

"I don't even have a proper name."

Fern's grandmother was using silver tongs to hand out ice from a bowl. She also set out a tray of little cakes (peach flavored) with flowers iced on top of them. The old big-game hunter started in on the cakes right away. One after the other disappeared under his moustache.

"We should call him Bixie," Howard said.

"Why?" said Fern. "Who would want to be called that?"

"He just looks like a Bixie. Good old Bixie!" Howard said defiantly.

"No, no," Fern's grandmother said. "Don't name

him, or he won't be general anymore. He'll be specific, and he won't be able to go back into the dictionary where he belongs."

The big-game hunter teared up suddenly. He looked like he might cry, in fact. But he popped three more cakes into his mouth, brushed his waxy mustache, sniffed twice and collected himself as if remembering that crying wasn't part of the definition of a big-game hunter, not one bit.

Everyone was quiet. The clock ticked in the parlor. Eventually the Miser and the Bone made an excuse about the giant peach pit being in an important thinking stage and how if they were to make any progress today, they had to get to it. They headed out to the backyard.

As soon as the big-game hunter had sipped his final sip, Dorathea told Fern and Howard to shake him back into the book.

Bixie said, "I could kill that rhino for you. I surely could. Most likely. I might. I can say with some confidence, not much really, that I could try. At least." He ate the last two cakes.

Fern's grandmother shook her head.

The big-game hunter sniveled. And Fern and Howard looked at Dorathea in such a way that said, *Do we have to shake him back into the book?*

Fern's grandmother took them aside. She whispered, "You don't want him to go wandering about outside of his dictionary. He'll lose his bearings. He could get stuck here, and he wouldn't fit in. He'd become a Nobody. You wouldn't want that, would you? You wouldn't want him to be a Nobody with no home, would you?"

A Nobody? Fern had never heard the term before. "But the hobbits do okay!" she said.

"Some truly prefer to be here, making a new home for themselves. But I don't think he will. He belongs in a dictionary. Being a Nobody, lost outside of your book, can be very hard on a character. Some find it truly painful. Being without a home is hard."

Fern remembered what it was like before she'd come to her grandmother's house. It was the first place that had ever felt like home to her. She loved it.

"Is that what you want to put him through?" her grandmother asked. "A desperate search for a home he's misplaced?"

"No," Fern said.

"Come on," Howard said to the big-game hunter. "The book's upstairs."

And so the three of them trudged gloomily up to the attic room. It was late afternoon now, and the room was hot with the trapped heat of the day. Howard sat down on the cot and so did Fern. The big-game hunter toured the room, looking at book titles, picking up books, thumbing through.

"So many books," he said in a shaky voice. "I had no idea there were so many."

This made Fern think of all the bottles that had plopped out of the book. In fact, she saw the bottle that Howard had held on to as some sort of keepsake sitting up in the sill of the high crescent window. "I wish I knew what to do about all those messages," Fern said, sighing, plopping down on the edge of Howard's bed.

"Messages? Oh, that's something I should know about. Sending messages from the jungle. I should know about that, shouldn't I?" the big-game hunter said dreamily.

"Maybe it's a prank." Howard picked up the dictionary. "Come on, Old Bixie!"

"Don't call him that," Fern warned, remembering what her grandmother had said.

But Howard didn't listen. "Come on, Good Old Bixie," he said again.

And this time the big-game hunter looked up. "What is it?"

"Time to get into the book," Howard said.

But Fern suddenly felt uneasy. "What's your name?" she asked the big-game hunter.

Without hesitation, the big-game hunter answered.

"My friends call me Bixie. Good Old Bixie."

Fern glared at Howard, and Howard stiffened up and glared back.

"What is it?" Good Old Bixie asked.

"Nothing," Howard said. Then to Fern, "Quick. Get him into the book." He shoved the book at her.

"About those messages," Good Old Bixie said, "you can send messages by bottle, sure, but pigeon is more efficient. The natives use smoke signals. Once, when on grand safari with Chief Otwatan—"

Fern opened the book hurriedly to the Bs, then placed it on the floor. "Sorry to interrupt. But we've got to go quickly now. You'll have to step into it like a pair of trousers, and I'll shimmy the book up around you until you're inside."

"I don't want to," said Good Old Bixie.

"But you have to!" Fern said.

"I don't want to, my dear," Good Old Bixie said again.

"There's no time to talk about it!"

"Where's my gun? I can't go back without my gun." Good Old Bixie didn't sound like the general idea of a big-game hunter anymore. He made this last statement with a strange twinkle in his eye that scared Fern.

"Oh, I'll shake it in after you," Fern said.

"I need my gun. I'm not going in without it."

Howard said, "We've got no choice. I'll go get it." And he ran down the stairs to get it.

Fern and Good Old Bixie just stared at each other. "It's hot in here," Fern said.

"I'm used to the heat of the jungle," Good Old Bixie said. "I feel right at home."

"You know this isn't your home. It can't be."

"I rather like it here."

Just then Howard bounded in with the ancient gun.

"Don't—" Fern began, because she was afraid of Good Old Bixie. She no longer trusted him. She had the idea that he'd turned into someone else, someone who knew what to do with a gun, especially an ancient one with a fluted barrel used in the jungle.

But before she could get out the rest of the sentence, Howard had handed the gun to Good Old Bixie, who, of course, took it and quickly spun it around and pointed it at them. (Now, I should mention here that it isn't a good idea to point a gun at anyone. I recently had the unfortunate experience of being shown a musket at an antique show while researching the outfit that Good Old Bixie wore so that I could give accurate details. And this musket, while being pointed at me, went off with a thunderous bang. It blew off a wedge of hair on the side of my head. Should I mention that the gun's owner, a Mr. Talmudge Peevish, had never ever loaded the gun?

And so how, you ask, did the gun get loaded? Was my crazy old professor to blame? Here we can all nod knowingly at one another.)

Howard and Fern froze, looking into the gun's big gaping mouth. Although Fern had faced all kinds of danger before, including a dinosaur, a tornado and most recently a rhinoceros, she'd never had a gun pointed at her. It was a different kind of fear altogether.

"I'm off to get a rhino," Good Old Bixie said. "Don't try to stop me. It wouldn't be wise."

"But . . . but . . . you have to get back into the book," Fern said. "You belong there. You'll have no home. You'll be a Nobody." The word "Nobody" echoed around the little attic. It was a sad, doleful word.

"So sorry, chaps," said Good Old Bixie. "I've got work to do here. And if I were you, I'd respond to messages the way they've come. If by smoke signal, then respond in smoke signal. If by pigeon, then respond by pigeon. If by bottle, then by bottle."

And with that farewell bit of information, the big-game hunter, not just the general idea of one, but this one in particular, this one named Good Old Bixie, backed out of the room and shut the attic door.

THE STORM 4

"WHO WOULD HAVE THOUGHT THAT GOOD OLD Bixie would turn on us like that?" Howard said nervously, wringing his hands. "Maybe he'll just wander off, and no one will have to know that we didn't get him back in the book."

Fern's heart was still beating hard in her chest. She was relieved that Good Old Bixie was gone. "We'll have to confess. What if they've already seen him walking out of the house with his gun? I can't believe you got us into all this trouble!"

"ME?" Howard shouted. "I was just reading my math books all by myself, very happily, until you came along! It's all your fault!"

"MY FAULT?" Fern shouted back.

"YES, YOURS!"

They didn't have time to argue the point further. (Which is probably just as well, as arguments like this can go on for hours. I once got into an argument with my creative writing professor—just before he began open hunting season on N. E. Bode. It was at a book event much like a writerly petting zoo where authors are seated behind little tables of their books and readers can come by and coo and, sometimes, pat the authors' heads. He said, "And you call yourself a *writer*!" And I said, "I do." And he said, "Well, stop!" And I said, "You stop." And he said, "No, you stop." And we went on like that for so long that I lost track of time and started day-dreaming about cheese and grapes—which is often what the authors are fed at these events.)

Fern's grandmother was calling. "Fern! Howard! Come quick!"

"She knows!" Howard whined. "We're doomed!"

But no, that wasn't it at all. This had nothing to do with Good Old Bixie and the rhino. With all the commotion, Fern and Howard hadn't noticed that the attic room had grown dark. A big thunderstorm was approaching. It had been building with the heat all day, and now huge gray clouds had swung in. A wind had picked up, tossing tree limbs about.

"Coming!" Fern called back.

As she and Howard reached the kitchen, the rain had already started. The Bone was hauling lobster pots from the cupboards and dumping the books out of them. He handed the pots to the Miser, who stood there looking frightened. The thunder crashed overhead and the Miser jumped, then shuddered. It was getting harder and harder to believe that he'd once been capable of any real action at all, much less evil.

Fern's grandmother was setting out some model ships,
handed down from Fern's
grandfather.

"How are those going
to help?" Howard asked.

"They're for the Bor-
rowers," Dorathea said. "I
always put them out when there's the possibility of a flood. They won't use them 'til we're gone. But you'll notice they'll be missing, and they always dock them nicely when they're done."

"What about the others?" Fern asked, thinking about the Indian who lived in the cupboard and the hobbits.

Dorathea nodded to the countertop, where the

Indian was fashioning a raft from wooden spoons and twine. "The hobbits will climb up on the tops of their houses and onto their chimneys if the water gets too high out there." Fern's grandmother gave Howard and Fern two mop buckets. "Take these upstairs. Put them under any leaks."

You see, a roof made of books isn't the best way to keep rain out—not even if the books are sturdy library-bound editions. Usually Fern's grandmother used her pots to catch leaks when heavy rain seeped through bindings and started dripping. But this time it was much worse. The rhino's pounding hooves and the big-game hunter's aimless gunshots had rattled loose books on the roof, leaving some real holes.

Fern and Howard ran upstairs. The thunder cracked overhead again. In each of the bedrooms, the ceilings pooled with water and dripped and then poured. Eventually the leaks were slipping through the walls, along hidden beams, and puddling downstairs as well. It became a race, placing buckets and pots under leaks, dumping the water out the windows and then replacing them. It was fast, hard work, and it took everyone helping—Fern, Howard, the Bone, the Miser and Dorathea.

The lights flickered, then dimmed, then failed. The electricity had been knocked out by a tree that had fallen on the lines along the main road. Lightning shot through

the windows in bright flashes, and finally lightning was
the only light to see by. The storm kept up. They worked
through dinner and into the night.

Eventually exhaustion set in. Dorathea called a meeting in the upstairs hallway. The rain was so loud that
she had to shout to be heard above it. "We'll take turns
sleeping. There's not much of a leak above the Miser's
bed! If you sleep with a bucket on your chest, I think
you'll find the rest of the bed is kind of dry! Once the
water in the bucket is too high and begins to spill, then
it's the next person's turn to sleep!"

And so it went.

Howard was first. He was the guest, after all. It was the least they could offer. Fern watched him put a metal trash can on his chest and close his eyes. She was still angry at him for not having let go of the book with the rhino stampeding out of it and for shaking out a big-game hunter to try to fix things. But now he looked so peaceful, so little and damp. The raindrops were pinging against the bottom of the metal garbage can. *Howard!* she thought. What could she do with him? And she felt a sort of sweet pang. It almost was a pang of love, but Fern refused to believe it. So she decided it was a pang of annoyance instead. "That Howard!" she said, shaking her head.

She went back to work. Time passed. Fern was weary. Her arms ached. She was soaked. She still wanted to confess about Good Old Bixie. Maybe it was guilt, not just wet clothes, that was weighing her down. She felt guilty about the whole thing. But there was no time to get her grandmother's or her father's attention.

Fern's grandmother caught her in the hallway. "Where is the Miser?" Dorathea shouted. "I sent him for flower-pots and he isn't back yet!"

"I can go and get flowerpots!" Fern shouted back.

"They're in the basement!"

And so Fern jogged down the stairs, where a small

waterfall had formed. (Do I even have to mention that I was recently pushed over the WachiHachi Waterfall while on a crowded guided tour and that the pusher was never found? I survived but am now afraid of my shower and only take baths wearing a life jacket.) The water had inched up the books piled against the wall. Fern splattered through the kitchen, where she noticed that the miniature ships were, in fact, gone. She stole a glance into the living room, where she was sure she saw one of the masts and the end of one ship slip behind the curtains. She decided to let the Borrowers anchor there without interruption. They so hated to be seen!

Fern walked back to the kitchen and opened the door to the basement. There was another small waterfall trickling down the basement stairs. Fern was about to make her way to the knee-deep pool below when she heard voices in the basement. She stopped. She squatted down and tried to make out what was being said and who was saying it.

"A deal's a deal," someone was saying angrily. "How many times do I have to remind you that it's time to pay up. I did it for you, you know. I got the Bone behind bars, and now you owe me. When I got word that you'd been defeated by the Great Realdo and an eleven-year-old girl, I knew that the Great Realdo and this girl were linking up. I knew that the book existed, safe and sound,

55

and that it was a force between them. Look what they've reduced you to! A quivering mouse of a man. It's my turn, Miser. I have my own needs for the book, and they aren't about some woman who done me wrong. I have real reasons!"

Fern slipped down another step and peered into the dark basement, but she couldn't get a wide enough view. The voices were bouncing around, but she couldn't see anyone.

"Just give me more time," the Miser said. His voice was shaky, timid and exhausted. "I need time. I don't know what to do. I'm not the way I used to be. Please, please!"

"You said you'd get rid of the girl, you'd get the book, and I would be able to have the crown and scepter! And I would be in my rightful place. I want my title! I want what is rightfully mine! I want my legacy! You've befriended these people. You can get your hands on the thing, and if you don't cooperate, I will start to do harm, I can tell you that. I'll give you one day, and after that I will start to do harm! Harm, I tell you! Grave harm! Don't you tell a soul about this, Miser. Do you hear? Not a soul. Just give me what's mine!"

And then Fern heard a paddling sound. She saw a fat mole. No, not the kind of mole that shows up near the rosy nose of a postal clerk. No, no, no. A mole, you know, the kind of animal that burrows and doesn't see too well. This one was enormous, as fat as a fat cat, and it had a giant flower-shaped nose—two big blooming nostrils. It was sitting in a small wooden bucketlike boat, paddling with its paws across the flooded basement. It was wearing a backpack filled with things that clunked together, dull chimes. The backpack was heavy and awkward and made it difficult for the mole to stay on course. It made its way toward a small hole in the dirt wall. "Grave harm!" it barked one more time over its shoulder and then disappeared into the hole.

Fern stood up quickly and dashed to the kitchen. She didn't want to get caught spying. She saw the Indian on his raft. He was poling along. He seemed peaceful, which only made Fern feel less at peace. He gave her a nod. She nodded back quickly and splashed upstairs. Her grandmother was in her bedroom dumping buckets. "He's coming," Fern said, "with the pots!"

"It's about time!"

Just then Fern heard a scream, a sharp gasp, really, coming from the Miser's bedroom. She and her grandmother and the Bone all ran toward it. The Miser was the only one not to show up. There was Howard. The garbage can on his chest had overflowed, waking him up. It was a hard way to wake up.

"Are you okay?" the Bone asked.

"Yes, dear, is something wrong?" Dorathea added.

"I thought I was drowning. I was dreaming of trouble," Howard said, looking pale and terrified and sopping. He rubbed his eyes and slipped off the soggy bed, handing Fern the garbage can.

"I think we may be in trouble," she said under her breath, thinking of the mean, fat-cat, flower-nosed mole while she poured the water from the garbage can out the open window.

"It's your turn to sleep, Fern," Dorathea said.

"Sweet dreams," said the Bone.

Fern was waiting for Howard to say something to her too. But he didn't. He just walked out of the room, rain dripping down on his head.

TO WHOM IT MAY CONCERN

FERN DROPPED ONTO THE BED AND POSITIONED the metal can on her chest. At first the drops seemed too loud, like a gong in the bottom of the empty bucket, and she thought she would never fall asleep. She was thinking about the flower-nosed mole. What had he said? What was his legacy? What was this title he was after? And, mainly, was he really the one who'd put her father in jail eleven years ago, not the Miser? Fern knew the book he wanted—*The Art of Being Anybody*. And Fern knew where it was, safe and sound under her mattress. But how could it produce a crown? Isn't that what the mole had said? He wanted the crown? His legacy? She kept thinking about the mole and the rhino wandering out there, Good Old Bixie hot on its trail, and the water everywhere, raining down. Soon the gongs became gentle plops as the water filled the can's bottom. The rain on the roof was loud and steady. The thunder had died down. Fern's eyes closed and she was asleep.

She was dreaming of her mother on a boat. The sun was shining, and her mother was laughing. Fern was in the boat with her. Maybe they were in Africa somewhere. There were hippos with those birds sitting on them and rhinos and elephants surrounding this water hole where the boat floated. And the boat was made of the peach pit, of course. It was Fern's father's handmade boat, complete with white sails.

Fern was telling her mother the story about that very night, about the rain coming in everywhere. It was a funny story now, and her mother laughed along. Then she touched Fern's arm. "Look," her mother said, "a school of bottle fish!" And Fern looked and saw a Diet Lime Fizzy bottle and then another, and then the water was filled with Diet Lime Fizzy bottles. Her mother caught one in her hands, and it was a fish, a green bottle-nosed fish with the Diet Lime Fizzy logo shining on its scales. "What do you have to say for yourself?" her mother asked the bottle fish.

"Help us, Fern! Save us! Are you listening? This is urgent! Fern, save us!"

Fern's mother turned to her. "You have to save them, Fern. I can't, but you can, my dear. You can."

Fern opened her eyes. The dream disappeared. She sat upright, knocking over the garbage can of water, which splashed down her legs and all over the bed. "I've got to save them!" she said. She got out of bed and opened the bedroom door. She peered down the hallway in each direction. It was empty. She could hear the others sloshing through the distant rooms. She walked to the small door at the end of the hall that led to the short stack of attic steps and Howard's bedroom. There, floating on the water that had poured in through the ceiling and down the little stairs, was the Diet Lime Fizzy bottle that Howard had held on to. Fern grabbed it, charged up the steps and into Howard's room. She rummaged through Howard's small desk drawer for a pen, and, deep in the middle of a stack, she founded some dry pages. She wrote on one of the pieces of paper in a smeary scrawl: *To Whom It May Concern: Who are you? And what do you need? Fern*

She quickly shoved the note into the bottle and pulled a book randomly from the shelf. A book on fishing, in fact, and fisheries. She placed the bottle on an open page and shook it until the bottle slipped into the pages. *What now?* Fern thought. *What should I do now?* But she didn't have long to wait. People were calling her name.

"Where are you? Fern! Miser?" again and again. It was Dorathea and the Bone and Howard. The voices seemed to be echoing throughout the house.

Fern found Howard in the upstairs hallway.

"There you are!" Howard said breathlessly.

"Of course here I am. Where should I be?"

She could hear the Bone's and Dorathea's voices echoing downstairs, still calling for her and the Miser. "What's wrong?"

"The Miser's gone. He was supposed to bring pots

from the basement, but he never did. And then Dorathea looked in his bedroom. You were missing and so were his clothes, his bag, his letters, everything packed up and gone."

Fern ran to the Miser's room, which was indeed empty. Then she ran to her own room. Howard followed. She walked to her rain-smeared window and looked out. The hobbits' underground homes must have been flooded too. They were perched up on their grassy roofs, just like Dorathea said they would be. Beyond them Fern saw a figure wading off into the watery distance. They had worked through the night and now the sun was coming up, though it was barely noticeable through the thick bank of clouds. It was still drizzling. She opened her window. "Miser!" she yelled. "Miser!"

The Miser didn't look up, but, drawn to the sound of her voice, the Bone and Dorathea stepped out of the front door and looked up at her. "There you are!" they said. "Where's the Miser?"

Fern pointed out across the yard.

"Miser!" the Bone called as loudly as he could.

The Miser finally turned around. He looked at the house. His expression was desperately sad.

"He has to go," Fern said quietly.

And then she yelled to him. "There's a rhinoceros out

there, and a crazy hunter with a gun. Be careful!"

The Miser looked up at the window and nodded solemnly. Fern and Howard and the Bone and Dorathea watched him slosh out beyond the front yard. They watched him for as long as they could, until he was clean out of sight, and then, of course, Fern and Howard had to look down from the window. And there were the Bone and Dorathea standing on the front steps, arms crossed, looking up.

"And what?" the Bone said, fumbling, astounded.

"A crazy hunter with a gun?" Dorathea continued on. "You didn't get him back into that book?"

Fern and Howard exchanged looks. They had some explaining to do.

"Don't move a muscle," the Bone said.

"We're coming up to have a word with you," Dorathea said.

"Yes, okay, we won't move," Fern replied. She shut the window. "Howard!" she said, "there's so much to tell. A mole with this big nose like a flower threatened the Miser," she said, lifting up her wet mattress. Fern was relieved to find two books there—her mother's diary and *The Art of Being Anybody*. (Did it contain a crown? Certainly not in the pages Fern had struggled through.)

Fern stayed under the tent of the mattress and opened the books. Their covers were damp, but inside the pages were still dry, luckily. "That's why the Miser is gone and . . ." She quickly grabbed a book off the nightstand and shook it, hard and fast. A Fizzy bottle fell with a plop to the water at their feet. "And I wrote a note that said who are you and what do you want." She saw a note in the bottle and fiddled to get it out.

And just as the door was beginning to open, she read the note to Howard in a whisper: *We are Nobodies. We want to go home.*

BLIND AS A . . . *BUS DRIVER?*

FERN HEARD TWO SETS OF FAMILIAR FOOTSTEPS on the stairs—her father's march and her grandmother's shuffle. She exchanged a nervous glance with Howard, then dropped the mattress, which they both sat down on quickly as the Bone and Dorathea appeared at the door.

"What happened?" the Bone asked.

Fern's bed was soaked. She and Howard dangled their feet in the water as if they were fishing off the edge of a dock.

"How is it that the hunter isn't back in his dictionary?" Dorathea asked.

The Bone looked angry, but also a little lost and

confused. Fern figured he was wondering why the Miser was gone. Why had he left without saying good-bye? Dorathea wasn't pleased either. Fern didn't know whether or not to tell them about the evil flower-nosed mole in the basement. It had been so adamant that the Miser not tell anyone, *not a soul*. If Fern told the Bone and Dorathea, would it only make more trouble for everyone?

Howard answered quickly, telling the Bone about how he'd made up the hunter's name and suddenly he became more real, and how he turned the gun on them in the attic. "He's only after the rhino," Howard said, as if it really were no big deal to have a hunter tracking a rhino in these parts.

Fern sat quietly next to Howard, who was nervously swishing his feet around. The rain continued to drip from soggy patches in the ceiling, but the sun was up now, lighting up the Bone's and Dorathea's faces. Fern kept glancing at her grandmother. She wasn't angry and flushed like the Bone. She was calm, but there was a stitch in her eyebrows, which were crumpled up above her large eyes. It was an expression Fern had never seen before. It made Fern feel a little sick. She wanted to say that this was all Howard's fault. It wasn't fair that she was roped up in it! She decided to try to be helpful. "Good Old Bixie likes tea and cakes. Maybe you can lure him back with tea and cakes." Her grandmother's expression didn't change.

"I don't think they should be allowed to go to camp, Dorathea," the Bone said. "Camp is a privilege. If they don't deserve it . . ."

Fern was so frustrated that she felt like crying. She needed to go to camp! She needed to find people like her!

Howard said, "Good. I don't want to go. I'd rather be with Milton!"

"Milton!" Fern said. "Well, at least Beige Boy is more fun than you!" Actually, Fern was feeling pretty bad. Couldn't Howard pretend that going with Fern to camp wouldn't be torture?

"At least Milton is a normal kid!" Howard said. "Not like you . . . You're . . . you're . . ."

Fern didn't want to hear what awful thing Howard might say to her. She looked up at her grandmother. "I want to go to camp so that I can make some friends! I don't have any *real* friends!" She could feel Howard glaring at her, but when she glanced at him, he looked down at his hands. Maybe she'd gone too far.

"Well!" said Dorathea. "I think that they deserve to go to camp—with each other. I'm disappointed with the two of you." So that's what the expression was. Disappointment. Fern had never seen her grandmother disappointed before Howard started acting up. "I'm not so much disappointed about the rhino and Bixie, but, well, I think of you two as brother and sister, in a way. Don't you, Bone?"

"I do," said the Bone, nodding.

"You should be kinder to each other. I only had one child, Eliza, and she was lonesome, and she'd have loved to have a brother or a sister. Didn't you want to have a brother or sister back before you knew about each other?"

Fern had. For eleven years she hadn't known anything about Howard, and she'd always been jealous of the kids she knew who had brothers and sisters. She'd hoped and hoped and hoped for some kind of brother or sister to knock at her door. And that's what happened! She nodded. Howard did too.

"Here you are wasting it," Dorathea said.

Fern felt awful. In fact, she felt more than awful. She felt heartbroken, but still she wanted Howard to feel heartbroken too. She glanced at him, and he looked sad, but, well, she couldn't tell what kind of sad—the I'm-in-trouble variety or the truly regretful. And she didn't want to sound too sad if he wasn't really regretful. "I'm sorry," she mumbled.

"Me too," Howard mumbled.

"Well, it's time to pack up," the Bone said.

"Yes," Dorathea said. "Get your things together. The bus will be here soon."

Dorathea and the Bone walked out of the room, leaving Howard and Fern sitting there glumly. Fern wanted to say she was really sorry that they'd wasted their time fighting with each other, but she couldn't quite bring herself to. What if Howard made fun of her, or ignored her, or didn't believe her? She stood up and pulled out her soaking wet suitcase from under the bed.

"Are you going to bring your mother's diary?" Howard asked. This was, in fact, a thoughtful thing to say, and maybe a way of Howard coming around a little. Fern loved her mother's diary, even though she couldn't read it. Howard had been in charge of decoding the diary, but he'd had no luck. He'd returned the diary to Fern as soon as he'd shown up the week before. The diary wasn't in code. It was hypnotized, like *The Art of Being Anybody*, which could only be read by its owner. But with the diary, they didn't know who could read it or under what circumstances.

"Yep," Fern said, "I'm going to bring it."

"Maybe, one day, something will come clear and you'll be able to read it," Howard added.

"Yes," Fern said, disheartened. "Maybe."

Fern lifted up her mattress again and looked at the wet diary. The sight of the diary always shook her a little. She still was surprised by how much she loved her mother—a woman she'd never met. *The Art of Being*

Anybody was there too. It had to come with her as well, so it wouldn't fall into the wrong hands—like a pair of mole paws! Fern picked up both books.

"Did I ever tell you that strange thing that happened once while I was trying to decode that diary?" Howard said. "I was so sleepy that I'm pretty sure I dreamed it."

"Dreamed what?" Fern asked.

"I dreamed that I read an entire entry," Howard said. "It was blurry and hazy, but I could read it."

"What did it say?" Fern was anxious. Her heart was pounding away in her chest.

"It was about how your mother tried to help this girl, a girl who had a twin brother, how they'd come for a visit, friends of the family. And how she couldn't help the girl, and it made her feel useless and lonesome. But, you know, it made me feel better. I'd tried to help the Drudgers, and I couldn't really. They are who they are. I missed them as monkeys. And I was feeling useless and lonesome, but after I read the entry I felt better. But when I came to the end, I closed the book, and then I couldn't find that entry again, or any entry that made any sense at all."

Fern was jealous. She was thinking about her mother now, about her mother as a girl who wanted to help someone. It was strange to think that her mother had written all about it while in this very house, maybe while lying down in this very bed. Just then Fern remembered her own dream about her mother in the boat in Africa with the Diet Lime Fizzy bottle fish, and how her mother had looked at her . . . *"You have to save them, Fern. I can't, but you can, my dear. You can."* It had been so real, so vivid. Fern had looked through the diary every night, hoping that something would come clear to her. And it had never offered her anything.

"Well, that doesn't make any sense. Why would the diary be hypnotized under strict orders to let you, and only you, a stranger, understand an entry, only one entry, about some twin that my mother couldn't do anything to help? Why would my mother have hypnotized her diary so that it would reveal something like that to you?" Fern was angry at Howard again. She was still stinging from her grandmother's disappointed eyebrows. She didn't want to hear that Howard had been let into her own mother's childhood without her.

"I'm just saying what happened," Howard snapped back. "It was probably a dream, like I said."

"Yeah, probably."

Just then there was a horn outside. Fern still had her packing to do. Howard did too. "Is that the bus?"

"Must be," Fern said.

Howard rushed off to his attic room while Fern shoved things into her suitcase—some clothes, her toothbrush and floss. She stuffed *The Art of Being Anybody*, her mother's diary and her own diary into her backpack. She wanted to bring the messages from the Nobodies, too, of course, and so she shoved these in her pockets. Everything was waterlogged and extra heavy.

"It's here!" the Bone called out. "The bus!"

"Hurry! Hurry!" Dorathea yelled.

Fern swung her backpack up over her shoulder, dragged her suitcase to the window and looked out.

There was the bus. It was a sad bus. Yellow, of course, as buses tend to be. But it looked battered and bruised, like a banana that's been carried in a lunch bag for a week solid. It had the words "Camp Happy Sunshine Good Times" painted on the side, but even the bus didn't seem to believe it.

The doors squeaked open and a dog nosed out. It was a white dog with a spot of brown on one ear. The dog was wearing an orange safety jacket. Behind the dog, tapping down the bus steps with a long white stick, was the driver, a chubby, perturbed-looking man, wearing dark sunglasses and a little driver's cap. He had a big head, and his cap barely fit. In fact, it seemed to be pinching the man's head. On closer inspection from her bedroom window, Fern could see what was printed on the dog's jacket: "Seeing Eye Dog." (Should I say it? Should I even mention that I was recently

attacked by a Seeing Eye dog? It wasn't really a Seeing
Eye dog, because they are trained to be kind and loving.
No, it was a guard dog, a Chinese fighting dog, mas-
querading as a Seeing Eye dog. And who dressed this
dog in its tricky disguise? Who put this dog up to it?
Well, I think we all know who.)

Could it be that the bus driver, the man in the tight
cap, holding the white cane, was blind?

He took a few steps forward, then stumbled over the rough terrain of the front yard and cursed viciously until finally the dog barked in protest. The blind bus driver didn't seem to want to follow the dog's orders, but he did. He stopped cursing, folded up his white cane and frowned like a livid toad.

THE HERMIT WARNING

THE RATTY, BANANA-BRUISED BUS WAS SITTING there under the gray clouds. The blind bus driver held a clipboard tightly to his chest, arms crossed. He stood next to the Seeing Eye dog, both waiting in the drizzle.

Dorathea and the Bone hugged Howard and Fern.

"Have a good time," said the Bone. "I'm not worried about you two. You'll know how to take of yourselves." Fern was pretty sure that the Bone was thinking about the Miser, who probably couldn't take care of himself.

"He'll come back," Fern said.

The Bone nodded. "Oh, I'm sure he will. It just reminds me of how he took off all those years ago. He'd

81

pretended to be my friend right before the trial, you know. He was my alibi. And then he told them that I did it! I never stole anything from Auggie's Bait and Tackle!" The Bone's jaw was tense, the muscles hard as a knot. He'd never mentioned any specifics about his stint in jail before, and Fern had been too shy to ask about it.

"Of course you didn't steal anything from Auggie's Bait and Tackle!" Dorathea consoled him. "But the Miser is different now. Truly. He hasn't been pretending to be your friend again. He's been sincere. Don't you think?" She looked at the two children.

Fern and Howard nodded.

"What did they say you stole?" Fern asked. "What happened?"

"It was that old woman who accused me. I never went near the place! I don't even fish!" The Bone shook his head. "I don't want to talk about it!"

"Of course not," Dorathea said. "It's over and done with. You're a good man. An upright citizen! And the Miser will come back. I'm sure he has a good reason for having left."

Fern was sure he had a good reason too. She wanted to tell them that he was trying to protect them, but remembered the Mole's warning and kept quiet.

"Let's move, people!" the bus driver started shouting. "Let's shove off!"

Dorathea ignored him. "I remember when I went to this camp, years and years ago. It's where I first laid eyes on your grandfather, Fern," she said wistfully.

Fern hadn't heard much about her grandfather. There was a photograph of him on Dorathea's bedside table. He had kind eyes and a high forehead. He looked smart, with his mouth twisted just a little at one corner like he'd just told a joke and couldn't help but smile at his own cleverness. He'd died when Fern's mother was young. A war. Fern knew that much, and she wanted to hear more. But there was no time now.

"Move it out, folks!" the bus driver shouted.

He made Fern nervous. She picked up her bags. Dorathea was looking at the ugly bus, and the frowning driver and the spotted-eared Seeing Eye dog, who were too far away to hear anything.

"Is the bus driver blind?" Fern whispered anxiously.

"Yes," Dorathea said. "Too bad."

"He's blind and he drives a bus?" Howard asked, alarmed and with good reason.

"I heard that the regular bus driver never showed up this year and so they hired this new fella. Isn't it nice that he found work? It isn't easy for the blind to find good jobs," Dorathea said. "There's still a lot of discrimination against the disabled, you know."

Fern and Howard looked at each other, wide-eyed.

As I would. As you would. As we all would. As much
as we are for the rights of the handicapped, driving
buses may not be the best job for the blind. Even a
number of blind people whom I've interrogated on the
subject agreed. I've been afraid of buses ever since I was
nearly struck by one months ago. (I mentioned this incident in the opening letter—you did read the opening
letter, didn't you? In any case, you can imagine how just
writing about a bus—much less one driven by a blind
man—makes me very nervous. The memories are still so
vivid—my goodness, the grillwork, the shiny fender!)

The blind bus driver put Howard over the edge.
He'd been through a lot, you've got to keep in mind.
Even though he was a major source of the problems,
Howard wasn't much for this kind of excitement. He
really preferred order and calm. Howard began pleading, "I don't want to go! I really don't! Can I stay
here?" He glanced around at the house of books; the
yard of hobbit chimneys, where one hobbit still sat
dozing; the cornfield where Fern had last seen the
rhino. "I'll just stay in my room and read math books.
Really. That's all I want!"

Fern felt a little sorry for him.

"It's too late now," the Bone said. "And this'll be
good for you, Howard."

"Yes," Dorathea added, "and Fern needs you there."

"I don't need him there!" Fern said.

Dorathea handed Howard and Fern big bulging sacks of food. "It's a long trip," she said. "You'll need this for lunch and dinner, too."

Howard and Fern thanked her and walked off with their sacks of food. Fern could smell the peach flavoring. It made her wince.

As they walked toward the bus driver, the dog barked once, announcing them. The blind man was reaching out his hand.

Howard stepped up and the bus driver's hand found Howard's head. "You are?"

"Howard," Howard said with a little break in his voice. The bus driver gave him a little bit of a shaking and then reached out again.

Fern stepped forward. The dog was eyeing her and Howard, then looking around the yard and back up at the house. The dog was suspicious, Fern was sure, but she wasn't sure what exactly the dog was suspicious of. The bus driver patted Fern's head. He was gruff and he rattled her head roughly. Fern hunched down to get away from him.

"Who are you?"

"Fern," she said.

"What's wrong with you, kid? You seem small and sickly." Fern was almost hiding now behind the food sack that her grandmother had packed. The smell of peaches was up in her nose suddenly, and it made her cough. The bus driver put his hands on his hips. "That you coughing, sickie? Can't have any sickies! That's the rules!"

Fern didn't know what to say. She wasn't sick! But it seemed pointless to argue with the man. She looked back toward Dorathea and the Bone. It seemed like they were miles away now. They waved across the yard. Fern turned to Howard, who was frozen.

"You'll have to stay here if you're frail, you know." The bus driver was beginning to smile. He liked the idea of leaving someone behind. *He must not like kids,* Fern thought. Maybe he'd made up the rule. It was a silly rule. Was Fern supposed to follow silly rules?

Fern still hadn't said a word. And now the bus driver was asking again. "Tell me now! Was it you who coughed or not?"

The dog looked at Fern. It had deep dark eyes, smart eyes, if such a thing can be said about a dog. It jerked its head back and forth, meaning, Fern guessed, that she should say no, that she didn't cough. But then who did? The dog nodded to itself, as if answering Fern's question. The dog coughed? Fern pointed at the dog. The dog nodded vigorously.

"No, I'm not sickly," Fern said. "It was the dog."

"The dog?" the bus driver said.

The dog barked, answering yes. "Oh, well then." He turned to the dog, defeated. "Okay then, nothing we can do about a sick dog. I guess that's that."

Fern smiled at the dog, and the dog smiled back. Howard and Fern climbed the bus steps, followed by the dog and the bus driver, still a little huffy. The bus was empty. Fern and Howard passed a few seats and then sat down one in front of the other. Their windows looked back at the house, and they both waved as the bus driver started up the growling motor. Dorathea and the Bone waved back as the bus headed down the long driveway to the open road.

Howard then looked at Fern like he had a brilliant idea. His face was all lit up. His finger was poised in the air. He started coughing, hacking, wheezing, all fake as can be. "Excuse me, sir, bus driver, sir," he sputtered. "I'm not feeling well! I think I have a terrible cough!"

"I should have told you out there, but this is another rule. Once you're on the bus, there's no turning back!"

Howard let out a sad little croak.

The dog barked once, and the driver came to a stop at a stop sign. She barked again once the road was clear, and he started up, straight ahead. "I'm Watershed, Gus Watershed. I'm the camp's bus driver and handyman," the bus driver said. "And this here Seeing Eye dog don't have a name. It's just a stray." The dog was leaning up against the dashboard next to the steering wheel. She nodded at Fern and Howard and then put her eyes back on the road.

Fern said "Hi" and Howard said "Hello" nervously, their eyes glued to the dog and the windshield and the road that lay before it.

"I bet you're nervous about camp. Well, let me tell you this. . . ," Watershed said. The dog growled softly, and Watershed veered around a curve to the left. She growled loudly, and he curved to the right. "You should be nervous. In fact, you should be scared." Watershed was a fast driver. A very fast driver, and very confident, especially for a blind person driving a bus. The road was rough and bumpy, and the landscape was zipping past the window. The dog was keeping up with the twists and turns with growls and barks.

"What should we be scared of?" Fern said, trying to sound calm, although she wasn't.

"You should be scared of that old Hermit. You should stay away from her and her hermitage and all of it," Watershed said. The dog turned back and looked at Fern with knowing eyes, but this time Fern wasn't sure how to read them.

"I'm not scared," Howard said, reaching over the seat, grabbing Fern's arm and staring at her with a look that said, *What are we going to do? Get us out of here!*

"Who's the Hermit?" Fern asked.

"No need for you to know about her. I shouldn't have told you. The less you know, the better," Watershed said.

Howard hummed nervously. Fern hummed back. The dog gave the equivalent of a dog's hum—to be a part of the anxious discussion—but this made Watershed turn right, turfing the nice little lawn of a very angry gardener, an old lady in white tennis sneakers. The dog growled enough to get Watershed to veer left, taking out a mailbox and plopping back down onto the main road.

"One more stop for this run," Watershed said, unfazed by the damage. "Corky Gorsky, to meet us in the parking lot of the Stop, Shop 'N Save. Nearly there."

They'd driven out of the country now and were in a popular part of town. Ah, the glam and glitter of strip malls! The genius of a year-round Christmas shop next to a cheese emporium next to a store solely devoted to wicker. I love strip malls—Christmas and cheese and wicker, too!

It was a huge relief when Watershed pulled the bus to a stop at the corner of the strip in front of the Stop, Shop 'N Save. Howard was looking greenish, and he obviously needed some stillness to regain his composure. Fern was queasy too, and the peach fumes from the lunch bags weren't helping any.

The Stop, Shop 'N Save was a humble little run-down

store that sold ordinary things, not giant Santas or imported, extra-baked, salted feta or wicker spittoons. No, it sold simple sundries, notions—milk quarts, chips, deodorant, striped gum, sour dills, wart remover. And standing in front of the Stop, Shop 'N Save was a boy. He was wiry and pale and a little freckled. He had that kind of papery skin that showed the blue of his veins underneath. He was bluish in fact. But he was standing up very tall and straight and stiff, like a little cadet, though everything about him seemed to say, *No, no, not a cadet*. He had a big Band-Aid stretched over his nose, flattening it to his face, which gave him a look of vulnerability. He had a little brown suitcase, the kind that might seem more suited to a very old man with knobby knees and Bermuda shorts waiting in a train station, but he wasn't a little old man with knobby knees and Bermuda shorts. He was Corky Gorsky. He looked like he was about to salute.

Watershed opened the doors. "Anybody there?" he asked the stray dog.

She barked a yes.

Watershed shouted, "That you, Mr. Corky Gorsky?"

"It's me, all right," Corky said. "Yes sir! Reporting for . . ." But then he stopped himself and smiled at everyone. "Yes, it's me. That's what I meant."

"Climb aboard," Watershed said.

"Ahoy," Corky said, walking up the big steps.

"I'm Gus Watershed," Watershed said, "and this here is my Seeing Eye dog, and in the seat there you have Howard." Howard waved. "And Fern. They're both fairly sickly, if you ask me."

Corky walked by the dog quickly and then looked around. He was a little confused, because Fern and Howard didn't look particularly sickly. Fern shrugged and smiled. Howard hummed again nervously.

"Hi," Corky said, and then he sat down.

As the bus started up, Corky began asking questions. "Where are you from? What do you like to do in your spare time? Are you looking forward to camp? What's your life like back home?" He was asking Fern and Howard so many questions that they didn't really have time to answer. Howard tried to say that he wanted to be at home with the Drudgers or at math camp or reading math books, but Corky didn't stop to listen. He fired the questions so quickly that Fern and Howard stopped answering and just let him keep asking question after question. He didn't seem bothered by the fact that the bus driver was blind and had a Seeing Eye dog. Maybe he was too busy trying to look, well, official, too busy trying to bombard Fern and Howard with questions, to notice.

Fern and Howard forced down their lunches as best as they could while Corky kept going with the one-sided interrogation. Finally, at a moment when Corky seemed breathless, Fern jumped in and asked a question. "So where do you live?"

Corky was stunned by the question. He babbled a little and then said, "I'm regular. My family is regular. My father isn't well known at all. And, no, I'm not going to tell you how my nose got busted. I don't remember, okay?"

92

Fern hadn't been expecting this. She wasn't going to ask him about his nose anyway. But now, of course, she thought that Corky Gorsky *wasn't* regular and that his father maybe *was* well known and that he *did* remember how he'd busted his nose and simply didn't want to talk about it because it was a bad story, maybe an awful story. She decided that Corky Gorsky asked so many questions because he didn't want to talk about himself.

Astonishingly, the sudden burst of his own information only slowed Corky down for a second or two. New questions flooded in.

Fern slid back into her seat. The bus was hot. It chugged and zigzagged along, guided by the dog's barks and growls. Howard looked sleepy. He'd rested his head on the window and now gazed out. Fern was deeply tired. She wanted to sit next to Howard and lay her head down on his shoulder, but she was sure he'd shrug her off. Fern put her half-eaten peachy lunch on the bus floor. She checked on *The Art of Being Anybody*, her mother's diary and her own diary by slipping her hand into her backpack. It was a nervous gesture, completely unnecessary, but it made her feel better to know just where they were. Now she felt her eyes get heavy, and her head dipped to her chest. Finally, lulled by the drone of Corky Gorsky's lullaby of unanswered questions, she lay down on the vinyl seat and fell completely asleep.

AND . . . MOLE HOLES

FERN WOKE UP TO A SHOCKING SIGHT. CAMP Happy Sunshine Good Times was dismal. The bus pulled onto a rutted road. There was a little faded sign on a warty piece of wood nailed to a tree: "*THIS WAY TO CAMP HAPPY SUNSH*"—and here the letters grew tiny because the person writing the sign realized that the piece of wood was too small and so they petered out—"*INE GOOD TIMES.*" It was only late afternoon, but the forest made everything dark. There were giant spiderwebs with toads bouncing through them. Fern could see them from the bus window. The webby woods ran alongside the road and then there was an opening, a worn-down circle surrounded by a stack of charred wood. There were twelve little cabins: five marked "Boys" (and labeled A through E), five marked "Girls" (labeled A through E), one marked "Boy Counselors" and one marked "Girl Counselors," but obviously these signs were written by the same person put in charge of the entrance sign. On both of the boy and girl counselors' signs, "ounselors" was written in tiny print. These cabins all leaned together in a tippy, off-balanced sadness.

When Fern looked in the other direction, things only got worse. Tucked out of the way was a small cabin with a red cross painted on its sign. Obviously this was where you were to go if you got sick. The fact that it was right next to the mess tent wasn't comforting. Fern knew that a mess tent meant that this was where they would eat, but mess tent seemed like the perfect name for it. Its screen door was ripped, its gutters swung low. It had a ratty paint job. If Watershed was the handyman, he wasn't very handy. Even if he couldn't see the disrepair, couldn't he hear the squeaking boards and smell the rotting wood?

On the other side of the mess tent was the smallest cabin. It had "Handyman and Bus Driver" (again not enough room for the "iver" in "Driver") and on the next line, "Gus Watershed." It, too, was on the verge of collapse.

The only thing that looked happy, sunshiny or good times about the whole place was a beautiful, very modern house that sat just off to one side. It was so fully air-conditioned that, once Watershed turned off the bus engine, Fern could hear it buzz. It had a gold-plated sign that swung from a metal post in the breeze. It read in properly spaced letters: "HOLMQUIST, CAMP DIRECTOR." Fern wasn't sure what she'd been expecting, but this

THIS WAY TO CAMP HAPPY SUNSHINE GOOD TIMES

wasn't it. Did gurus live in fancy houses?
Maybe so! She'd never met one before.

Why had her grandmother sent her to
such a place? Had it once been less
awful? Less toad filled and funky
smelling? In the distance she
could see a murky pond. What
was that frothing up
from it? Was that
where the
awful smell

was coming from? And why were there holes all over the ground? It would be hard to walk without losing a foot down a hole and twisting an ankle.

Gus Watershed turned around. "Well, here you are!"

No! Fern wanted to shout. *I won't go!*

She looked at Howard, and he looked like he'd received an electrical shock. She looked at Corky Gorsky, and he looked like he wanted to cry but was refusing to. He rubbed his nose, nearly upsetting his Band-Aid.

Now out of the cabins there were kids walking (tripping and stumbling over the holes), coming to greet them at the bus . . . to greet them? Or to eat them? Some seemed menacing. Some looked miserable. A few of the older ones looked especially mean, the ones creeping out of the counselors' cabins. Some of these counselors had, oddly enough, dog ears, cat tails—one girl had the face of an angry racoon. Anybodies, Fern thought, who'd been caught midtransformation. One boy had a beak!

Fern had been prepared to rough it a little. She expected some of the staples of camp life that apply to all camps (even math camp from her days as the Drudgers' daughter)—outdoor toilet facilities, rickety shower stalls, mosquito repellent, and a beverage called bug juice, which attracts bugs that often end up swimming in your cup. But this! No. What could have prepared her for this? (I myself never went to camp. The Axim School for

AND . . . MOLE HOLES

the Remarkably Giftless is year-round. I asked a lot of people about camp experiences, and I did a lot of solid research in dusty libraries. And in one of those libraries I narrowly escaped a domino effect of falling library bookshelves, but let's not even get into that now. But in all of the stories I've heard of camp misery, I've never come across a place as horrible-sounding as Camp Happy Sunshine Good Times.)

Gus Watershed opened the bus door. The dog wriggled out of her Seeing Eye dog jacket. She looked at Fern and gave her a wink. Fern, of course, winked back. The dog then bolted down the steps across the opening and into the woods. Fern didn't blame her. The woods were safer, weren't they? Still, she immediately missed the stray Seeing Eye dog. *Don't go!* Fern thought. *You're the only one I trust!*

Watershed turned angrily to the kids. "Okay, everybody off."

But Fern and Howard and Corky didn't budge.

Fern wanted to find a quiet corner and disappear. Fern wanted to shake a message in a bottle into a book. It was her turn to need some saving. Fern was pretty sure she was in danger.

Watershed reached behind the driver's seat. He picked up a cooler, opened it and pulled out a fresh bottle of none other than, you guessed it, Diet Lime Fizzy Drink.

99

Was this a sign? Did this mean something? Was there some link between Gus Watershed the blind bus driver and the Nobodies? Or was it just a coincidence? Diet Lime Fizzy Drinks are not all that popular, you know. All of these thoughts poured through Fern's mind. As he guzzled, Fern stared at him so sharply that even though he was blind, he seemed to feel her energy. He stopped drinking and said, "What? What is it? Somebody say something?" He swiveled his head around, listening. No one spoke. "Well, get off the bus now," he said. "Go!"

"Well," Corky said, "we're tough enough, aren't we?" But he didn't seem to believe they were tough enough. He seemed to break down for a moment. He said, "This isn't looking so good, is it?"

It was the first question of his that Howard and Fern had answered in a long time. "Nope," they said.

And the three of them stared out the bus windows at the frightened kids gathering by the door. A bunch were crowding in the door now, pushing at one another to climb the steps.

One said, "Excuse me, Mr. Watershed . . ."

Another was more to the point. "Take me home, please!"

A small chorus piped up. "Home! Home!"

"Get down now!" Watershed snapped at them. "Shape up! No need for lily livers!"

The kids got down off the steps, stumbling backward into the crowd.

Gus Watershed turned to Fern, Howard and Corky, and he gave them one more warning. "Watch out for them mole holes," he said, rubbing the cool Diet Lime Fizzy Drink bottle across his forehead. "If that mole's in one of them that you step into, he'll bite your foot but good!"

"*Mole* holes?" Fern said. "As in *moles*?"

"Yes, *mole* holes as in *moles*!" Watershed said snidely. "What are you kids, dense?"

And with that, the three kids sighed, climbed down the bus steps and moved toward the crowd of campers trapped in the glum, disturbing world of Camp Happy Sunshine Good Times, while Gus Watershed popped open another bottle of Diet Lime Fizzy Drink and gulped it down.

MARY STERN GETS WHAT'S COMING TO HER

MARY STERN INTRODUCED HERSELF AS FERN'S counselor. She had brown curly hair, little ringlets all over her head, and small teeth with metal braces on them. She talked very quickly and rarely took a breath. In fact, when Fern looked very closely at the side of Mary Stern's face, she saw little flapping gills, which might have actually made it easier for her to breathe while talking so much. She told them that Fern was going to join her girls' tribe and stay in one of the girls' cabins, and Howard and Corky would have to join Claussen Peevish's tribe and live with boys.

This separation was what Fern had been waiting for all week, but now that it was here, it was the worst news of all. She was scared as it was, and to have to go on alone seemed unbearable. But the separation didn't seem to bother Howard at all. He was muttering under his breath and it went something like this: "If I'd sworn off all this Anybody business when I went to the Drudgers' house, I wouldn't have turned them into monkeys and they wouldn't be afraid of me and I'd be sitting in their living room going over tax codes or discussing weed killer, which is where I belong, don't forget! But no. You've dragged me here, Fern. Right here!" Howard picked up his bag, ready to go.

Fern pretended that she didn't care either. "See ya later," she said, slapping Howard on the back.

Unluckily for Howard and Corky, it turned out that Claussen Peevish, their counselor, was the boy whose transformed face had a large, scary-looking beak, and he looked prepared to use it, too. (If you're wondering if there is any relation between Claussen Peevish and the antique musket owner Talmudge Peevish, the answer is no. It's just a strange coincidence. There are such things, you know.)

"You're late, Fern. Follow me. Come on. Let's go. We're in Girls' Cabin A. I've got to test you, see if there's anything you know. I've already tested your fellow tribeswomen." She pointed to three sour girls standing in front of the cabin door who looked like they'd been crying. Their eyes were red and their cheeks blotchy. "They don't know how to do anything. Not anything. I said, 'Are you girls Anybodies, or what? Do you call yourselves Anybodies? Well, you shouldn't! You're terrible losers! That's what you are! And crybabies, too! I should send all of you to the Hermit! See what she does with you!'"

The Hermit? Fern remembered Watershed's warning. Who was this hermit? Why was she so terrible?

Mary didn't give Fern a chance to ask questions. She bellowed on like a foghorn. "I've been a counselor here for four weeks. Four weeks!" She held up four fingers so that Fern could better understand the number four. "I've gotten to a full transformation three times! Fish!" She pointed to the leftover gills on the side of her neck. "So of course, I know more than all of you new kids." She pointed to Fern and the three sad girls. "Counselors always know more than campers. Always. Still, you would think that my campers would know something about being an Anybody! Something! But no. Each week a new set, and each week they don't know a thing!" She was exasperated, but somewhat happy, too. She seemed almost gleeful that her campers were, supposedly, idiots.

The doorway to Girls' Cabin A was flimsy and

screechy with a weakened spring. In fact, the spring was so weak that the door would hang open unless you slammed it. Mary explained this and slammed it. She told Fern to put her bags on the bottom bunk next to the window. Fern put her suitcase there, but left the backpack on so that *The Art of Being Anybody* and the diaries would be with her at all times. Mary then introduced Fern to the other three girls. Golgatha Beechum was heavyset, with droopy blue eyes and thin lips, and as Golgatha walked over to her bunk, Fern saw she had a limp in her right leg. Dolores Laverne Zabielski wore her hair in two long braids that were then wound elaborately on the top of her head, where they stayed in place secured by a very high number of bobby pins. She had one eye that didn't seem to open at all. Hester Measlette was bright eyed and had a short, blond pixie haircut. She was the only one of the three who didn't seem to have any impediments.

All the girls were scared of Mary Stern, and although Mary Stern was clearly mean, Fern could feel a little fire starting up in her. She refused to be bossed around by Mary Stern. She'd have to stand up for herself! Fern was steeling herself for a battle of wills. She could see it coming.

The cabin was damp and smelled a little like wet socks. The two sets of bunk beds sagged. They were tightly made with thick wool blankets on top and flat pillows. The windows had limp screens. The lights were bulbs attached to the ceiling with little strings with small rusty metal tips. The other girls hadn't yet unpacked their bags. There were a few open cubbies that were supposed to work as dresser drawers, Fern figured. But maybe the other girls were still holding out hope that this would be temporary and that their mothers would soon be on the way to pick them up. Fern certainly hoped that she wouldn't be staying the full week.

"Here," said Mary Stern, handing Fern a gold watch on a chain, much like the same one that the Bone had used a long time ago when he'd tried to dehypnotize a man who'd turned into a rooster. "Why don't you hypnotize . . . hmmm . . ."

All of the girls were shaking their heads. "Not me," said Golgatha. "I've got this limp already from Dolores Laverne."

"Not me," said Dolores Laverne. "I've got this one eye that won't unwink!"

"N-n-n-not m-m-me," said Hester. "I—I—I . . ."

"We know what happened to you during hypnosis! You and that awful stutter!" Mary said. "For goodness sake! I told you bunch of sissies it'll eventually wear off!"

Fern figured that it was a trick of some sort. Mary Stern had figured out a way to get the girls to bungle the hypnosis just so they would inflict some impediment on one another. The girls were obviously nervous, too. Fern wanted to put them at ease. "I can honestly say that I don't have any idea how to hypnotize anyone in any way," she said. "So you can consider me a failure in that department. Let's just say I failed the test!"

"Oh," said Mary Stern. "The other girls didn't know

anything either, really. I mean I had to *help* a little, you know, make *suggestions*. I could do that for you. . . ," Mary Stern said sweetly.

The girls were still shaking their heads vigorously behind Mary Stern's back but were too afraid to speak. Fern knew all about the power of suggestion. Once she'd thought the Bone was being attacked by a giant, murderous spider because the Miser, back when he was a bad guy, had *suggested* that something like that might happen.

"No need. I fail!" Fern said, trying to avoid a real fight with Mary Stern.

Golgatha, Dolores Laverne and Hester all sighed.

"Well then, I have another test!" Mary Stern said.

The girls looked around in confusion and terror. Obviously they'd only been given one test. Fern felt a wave of dread.

"Here," said Mary Stern. She handed Fern a book on swamp animals. "How about you shake something from a book?" Again, she spoke in a very candy-sweet way. "It's okay if you've never tried this before. Really!"

"Um," Fern hesitated. Just recently she'd seen the trouble that a book with a stampede in it could cause. She didn't want an alligator in the cabin! But Mary Stern was looking at her so menacingly. She didn't want to give in again. She reminded herself that she'd taken on tougher customers than Mary Stern. She'd defeated the Miser, and she'd used her smarts to do it. Fern thought about it. Really, would an alligator come out of the book? Lately only one thing had come out every time she'd tried to shake a book—a Diet Lime Fizzy bottle.

"Okay," Fern said, taking the book, hoping the Nobodies had been saving up some messages for her.

Mary Stern pretended that someone had just called her name from the front yard. She hovered near the door. "What?" she said. "You need me?" She was ready to make a fast exit just in case. Fern shook, and the book felt a little heavy. *Not an alligator,* she thought, *please!* She shook a little more and then—relief!—a Diet Lime Fizzy bottle fell to the floor with a *cloonk* and rolled under one of the bunks.

Fern looked up at Mary Stern as if none of this made any sense to her—and, well, Fern was honestly confused about a lot of things: was Gus Watershed's Diet Lime Fizzy bottle a coincidence? Were the mole holes?

Mary Stern was staring at Fern, flustered and angry. "What was that?"

Fern shrugged. The three girls looked at Fern in amazement.

"Do it again!" Mary Stern demanded.

Fern did it again. The cabin floor was so tilted that this bottle, like the first, quickly rolled under the bunk and clunked against the other bottle. Now Mary Stern was really steamed.

"Do it again!"

Fern did it three more times with the same results. This was maddening to Mary Stern. Her face was sweaty. And, honestly, seeing Mary Stern this upset made Fern a little happy. It certainly made the other three girls happy.

"Let me have that!" Mary Stern said, grabbing the book from Fern.

"No," Fern said, "don't."

But it was too late. Mary Stern had already shaken the book with all of her might and, instead of bottles, three snapping turtles fell to the floor. Luckily they were all shut up in their shells. Mary Stern screamed. "What are you pulling here, Fern!" she yelled. "Reach into this!" And now Mary Stern stepped over the turtles and pulled a picture frame from her bag by the door. It was a picture of dirty worms. "Go on! It's okay if you've never tried this before either," she said, trying to regain her nice, fake singsong. "Try it. It isn't really gross. It's just a silly picture!"

Fern didn't mind worms, actually. The other girls were staring at Fern—Dolores Laverne with her one good eye. And so Fern reached in, but as she did, she chatted idly with Mary Stern. She said, "You know, you're quite lucky you haven't been hypnotized like the other girls—a limp, a permanent wink, a stutter. Those things can happen so easily. You're very lucky. You were standing right here and you could have wound up with all three!"

"Don't be silly!" said Mary Stern. "I'm a *counselor*!"

Fern's hand was deep inside the painting. She felt dirt and maybe a few worms, but mostly she felt the cool side of a bottle, and when she pulled it out, her hand caked with dirt, she brushed its side with her other hand—a Diet Lime Fizzy bottle.

"What?" Mary Stern was really angry now. She grabbed the bottle out of Fern's hand. "How did you do that? H-h-how did you do that?" The girls all stared at Mary sharply. Had she just stuttered? "D-d-did you ever d-d-do that b-b-before?" She was so angry that her face had gone red. One of her eyes was curling down in a grimace. She stormed around the room. "T-t-tell me how you d-d-did that! NOW!" But in the commotion, no one had noticed that the turtles had ventured out of their shells and were now snapping. One clamped on to Mary Stern's sandal and then another snapped at her big toe, getting in a sharp bite. "OW!" she howled, grabbing her foot, swinging the turtle clamped to her sandal around until it broke loose and whipped through the air and then through the screen of one of the windows. "OW!"

Just then Claussen Peevish opened the door. "Time
to meet for the lighting of the bonfire!" he yelled, his
beak wide and sharp as the turtles'.

Mary Stern pitched the bottle that was still in her
hand and it rolled, joining the others under the bunk.
She snapped at the girls, "Let's go! C-c-c'mon! M-m-
move, move, move."

It was awful, of course, but Fern felt triumphant.
Golgatha, Dolores Laverne and Hester followed Mary
Stern, who was wobbling with her hobbled gait. Fern
lagged behind long enough to stomp her feet near the

two remaining turtles so they'd pop back in their shells, and then she shook them back into the book. When she caught up with the girls, Golgatha's limp had disappeared. Dolores Laverne's eye had reopened. And Hester was whistling. Dolores Laverne walked up to Fern and said, "Wow, you really stuck it to her! I hope things are better now. It wasn't like this last year!"

"It wasn't?" Fern whispered.

Dolores Laverne was about to say more, but just then Golgatha hissed at her, "Dolores Laverne! Stay with us!" Golgatha was the most timid and frightened of the girls. Fern suspected that she'd figured out Mary Stern would have it in for Fern now, and Golgatha didn't want to get too close to such an obvious target. And so all Dolores Laverne had time to do was shake her intensely braided head and shuffle away.

Now Golgatha wouldn't look at Fern at all. But Hester Measlette raised her eyebrows and stared at Fern quizzically. She pointed to Mary Stern so that Mary Stern couldn't see and she mouthed, "Did you?"

Fern assumed she meant, *Did you hypnotize Mary Stern, suggesting the limp, the fallen eyelid, the stutter?*

Fern shrugged, but then also nodded a little, meaning, *I guess so, though I'm not really sure.* She'd never done such a thing, and actually she felt a little guilty about it. But only a little, because Mary Stern had been so rotten.

113

Mary Stern limped angrily around the maze of mole holes to the circle, where she sidled up beside Fern. With her one eye angrily pinched shut, she muttered, "I'll g-g-get you, F-f-fern!"

THE BONFIRE

ALL THE CAMPERS AND COUNSELORS HAD FORMED
a circle around a pile of logs and twigs. There was a lot
of chatter. Fern was keeping an eye out for Howard and
Corky, but she couldn't find them in the crowd. The first
thing that she did notice was that many of the counselors were drinking Fizzy Drinks. The campers weren't
given the privilege of drinking Fizzy products. They
were only offered bug juice from a big orange tank. (The
torture of mandatory bug juice for poor, thirsty campers
seems to be an unwritten rule of all camps.) Gus Watershed was there too, standing alone in front of his small
cabin, drinking a bottle, his little cooler at his feet.

He had his white stick. The dog wasn't with him. Fern missed the dog, especially now that Mary Stern had it in for her. Fern wasn't sure why, but she felt that the dog had been watching out for her.

Fern wanted to sit with the girls in her tribe, but they had held hands and long since skirted away. Fern walked along the outskirts of the circle. As she passed the recycling bin beside the mess tent, she noticed it was filled with empty Fizzy bottles.

Mary Stern was talking to her fellow counselors. Fern watched them. Mary Stern was retelling the story. She was pointing at her eye and she was rubbing her toe and she was looking through the crowd for Fern. Fern tried ducking and dodging behind the other campers, but it was no use. Mary Stern spied her. She narrowed her one good eye. The other counselors, three sharp-faced girls with their bony arms crossing their chests, sneered at Fern.

Fern did some more ducking and weaving and ran smack into Howard and Corky. Fern wouldn't have ever guessed that she'd be so happy to lay eyes on Howard, but she was! And Howard was beaming. He was over-joyed. Fern had never seen him so happy. "Isn't this great?" he said to Fern with this bouncy, joyous voice—you know, the voice people pull out to boom greetings for the holidays. "Corky and I are having the best time! Corky is the best guy ever! And I think Claussen Peevish is the best camp counselor in the world!"

"What?" Fern asked, confused.

"I love it here!"

"You do?"

"I really do!"

Fern stared at Howard a minute. He didn't look right. In fact, he looked kind of odd.

She looked at Corky Gorsky standing next to him. Corky was the same—a papery, weak-looking kid with an anxious expression, a Band-Aid flattening his nose and a stiff, soldier way of pushing back his skinny shoulders. "Don't you like it here, Fern? What do you think? Has homesickness set in? What do you think of your counselor? And the other campers?"

Fern ignored Corky's questions. She concentrated on Howard. How could Corky have won him over so quickly? Fern wanted to know. She'd been trying to get him to like being with *her*. But he preferred the blandness of someone like Milton Beige or the tireless questioning of Corky Gorsky.

"What about you, Corky?" Fern asked. "Do you love it here?"

Again, Corky was startled to have to answer a question. "Umm, what do you think?" he said. "Shouldn't we spend more time together? You, me and Howard, you know?"

Fern didn't know what to make of this. She hadn't

made any real friends in her tribe, but the whole thing seemed so very strange. She couldn't put her finger on it. "Okay," she said quietly.

"Corky's the best!" Howard said, and then he hugged Corky Gorsky. He just opened up his arms and squeezed the little guy. Howard had never hugged Fern, and this affection for Corky, this outpouring, made Fern feel a little jealous. Corky stood there and smiled at Fern, like he'd never gotten a hug before in all his life and wasn't sure what to do with one.

"Something's wrong," Fern said. "You know, this camp wasn't like this last year."

"Like what?" Howard asked. "Perfect?"

"No!" she said. "It wasn't this strange last summer. Something's wrong here," Fern said again. "Really wrong."

"Nothing's wrong, Fern," Howard said. "Except you saying things are wrong."

"Okay," Fern said. "Enough. I get it."

Claussen Peevish held a torch that lit his sharp beak, green eyes and the feathers shining throughout his hair. It was now just starting to get dark. He called out, "Anybodies, Anybodies, one, two, three!"

The whole place fell silent. All of the campers and counselors sat down, cross-legged, on the ground in a circle. Claussen lit the bonfire. The little twigs caught

quickly, and the fire roared and the pieces of wood
snapped and hissed. (Do I even want to talk about fires?
No. Not even innocent bonfires. It just so happens that
I recently ordered a flambé dessert in a fancy restaurant, but when the waiter lit it at my table, the flames
shot up wildly, the waiter dropped the dessert and my
tablecloth caught fire, throwing the whole restaurant
into a panic. Luckily there were no real injuries except
at the next table, where an overgroomed and highly

hair-sprayed poodle got a little singed. It was that kind of fancy restaurant where patrons could dine with their overgroomed and highly hair-sprayed poodles. But I must keep writing about this bonfire. Important things happen.)

"Time to recite the Anybody Creed. If you don't know it, learn it. All together," Claussen said.

The counselors spoke up loud and strong, and the campers mumbled along as best as they could. Fern listened.

"Anybodies should incorporate wisdom, decorporate listlessness and veritable sloth while set reforth into the worlds to raise up the important, the exportant, the good, artistic, with allowances for abject whimsy, and wisely thusly abling us with perceptitude and others to cherish this science, this art, this mystery of existing, and mostiferously be fair with those we love, for furthermore and et cetera."

Oh, Fern knew who'd written this! There was only one man who wrote in just this way: Oglethorp Henceforthtowith himself, the author of *The Art of Being Anybody*, of which the only copy in existence was the one Fern now kept in the backpack strapped to her shoulders. This particular section didn't sound familiar, but the writing style of Henceforthtowith was unmistakable. How had this become the Anybody

Creed? Who had passed it on?

"That was really very bad! Learn the creed!" Claussen Peevish said. Of course, as there were no handouts of the creed, there was no real way to learn it. "Now for our camp meeting. Is there any old business that needs attending to?" He looked around.

One of the counselors, the one with the racoon face, said, "Nobody's seen the Mole all day. Maybe he's gone!"

"Well, that would be nice. I for one would be happy," said Claussen, who didn't seem like he could be happy about anything. How could Howard think he was the best camp counselor in the whole world? It wasn't like Howard to make such grand statements, especially after so little time. "Has anybody seen the Mole today? The mean one, that is."

Everyone shook their heads. Fern wanted to know what the mean Mole looked like. Did he have a flowered nose?

"Just in case he's still lurking around, everyone knows not to go wandering off into the woods. Plus, the Hermit lives just beyond there, inside of a tree. If you see a tree with a door carved into it, don't go inside!"

The campers all nodded vigorously. The Mole, the Hermit. Stay away from trees with doors. Got it. But Fern had to admit that she was somewhat curious to see

121

a tree with a door carved into it.

"Any new business?" asked Claussen.

Mary Stern piped up now. "I th-think that campers should have m-more respect for their counselors. And if s-s-some camper is acting up, we should be able to cast them out into the night. If they're a m-m-menace to the other people in their tribe, they should be kicked out of the cabin. They can sleep in the woods. Get attacked by the Mole and the Hermit! That would t-teach them!"

Claussen Peevish looked skeptical. His beady green eyes darted around. "I don't know if we could get away with that. What do you all think?" he asked his fellow counselors.

The campers rose up in their timid voices, a mild uprising like a chorus of little baby birds. "No, no, no!" they chirped. Fern was the loudest, "No, no, no!" She knew that she would be the first one kicked out of her cabin overnight. She didn't like this place in the daylight—all webby, toady, stinky, mole-holey. She knew she'd like it much much less in the dark. It seemed like a ridiculous rule! How could they kick kids out? It wasn't right!

The counselors were louder and tougher, like big fat angry geese. "YES, YES, YES!" they squawked.

"Well," said Claussen. "I don't make the rules here. We just go by the informal vote, and the counselors were louder on this issue. So the rule stands. As punishment, bad campers can be asked to leave the cabin for the night to make it in the wilds on their own." Claussen liked the rule. *He likes making rules in general,* Fern thought. But wasn't someone in charge? Wasn't there a grown-up around who kept some kind of order? Claussen said, "Okay now, any questions from the campers?" Claussen asked this question, but it didn't seem like he was expecting any volunteers.

Fern was nervous. She knew she'd be kicked out one of these nights—maybe even tonight. It wouldn't be possible to win Mary Stern over now. In fact, Mary was glaring at her at that very moment. But Fern wouldn't be intimidated. She'd overcome the Miser, she reminded herself again. She should be able to deal with Mary Stern. So she raised her hand.

Claussen was shocked. Had a camper ever asked a question before? "What? Do you . . . do you have a *question?*"

The campers' heads swiveled around.

"Yes," Fern said. All eyes fell on her.

"Are you sure?" he asked.

"Yes."

There was a wave of whispers.

"Okay, then. Go fast. Don't waste our time. Stand up."

She stood up. "I have two questions," Fern said,

although she really had three. Claussen sighed impatiently and glared. The third was about the Hermit, but Fern was feeling a little too afraid now to ask about her. And so she asked only the first two questions: "The first one is what does the mean Mole look like? How will we know he's the mean Mole and not just a regular mole? And also why is everyone drinking so many Fizzy Drinks?"

It was quiet for one second. Claussen was trying to form his answer. But then a voice rang out, a deep, low, sonorous voice. "These are good questions," the voice said. Everyone was wiggling around now to find the voice. From the shade of the big, modern house, a man in a gauzy white shirt and gauzy white pants appeared. He was wearing sandals, and his white hair was slicked back over his ears.

Claussen said, "Good evening, Mr.

Holmquist!" It was clear by Claussen's reverent tone that Holmquist didn't show up often and that when he did he was to be treated with grave respect.

"Good evening, Claussen," Holmquist said. He was wearing gold-rimmed glasses that sparkled in the bonfire light. "Let me explain. The Mole shouldn't be touched. Shouldn't be poked at with a stick. Shouldn't be talked to or whistled at. Leave the Mole alone. It has a giant nose. That's how it's different from a regular mole, and it is mean. It usually carries a backpack, which normal moles do not. It will try to bite you. It is very strong. Stay away from the Mole. And stay away from the Hermit's home, which is a tree with a door carved into it on the other side of the field." When he said this part, Fern felt like he was looking directly at her. She felt like he was giving her very specific directions, in fact, to the Hermit's house. Why would he do that while saying at the very same time to stay away from the Hermit's house? Fern wasn't sure what to make of Holmquist.

He turned to go, but he hadn't answered Fern's second question.

"What about the Fizzy Drinks?" she spoke up.

Holmquist turned. His smile was gone. He said in a low, gruff tone, "That's none of your concern." The campers twisted uncomfortably. The door to his house opened with a creak. Holmquist turned. An older woman was standing in the doorway. She nodded sharply to him, and when Holmquist looked at the campers, he gave them a large, toothy smile. "What I mean is: Fizzy is a special reward for our counselors and staff. We love Fizzy! Does that answer your question, Fern?"

Fern? Had he just called her Fern? How did he know her name?

Holmquist turned again and drifted past the gold sign that swung in the breeze: "HOLMQUIST, CAMP DIRECTOR." He walked up the stone path. The older woman opened the door for him and stared with slitted eyes at the children. The two of them disappeared into the arched doorway.

Claussen tried to regain the attention of the crowd. "Okay," he said. "Why don't we sing . . ."

Fern sat down. She wasn't listening. Now she knew that the Mole here was the very same mean mole who'd threatened the life of the Miser. But where was he? Could he be after the Miser again, doing him harm? Things were a terrible mess. And what had happened to Howard? Now he was singing his heart out, some dour marching song about allegiance. Fern could hardly stand it. And she didn't really trust Holmquist. The fact that he knew her name made him even more suspicious.

How did he know her? What had he heard about her?

Fern stared off into the trees. Beyond the cabins, off in the distance, she could see a small white shape shifting, pacing back and forth. It was a white dog with one brown-spotted ear. It was the stray Seeing Eye dog. She seemed to be watching the kids at the bonfire. She seemed to be keeping an eye on everything. Fern wanted to get up and leave the bonfire and go to the stray dog. She needed some help, and the dog seemed like the only one who'd be able to give it.

PART 3

NIGHT CREATURES

THE NEW RULE

MARY STERN HUSTLED THE GIRLS OF CABIN A through the mess tent. They sat on long wooden benches bristling with fat splinters. Fern choked down her cold hot dog wrapped in foil, watery macaroni and cheese and cubed Jell-O. She picked the bugs out of her bug juice and then, not too happily, drank it. Mary Stern barely ate any of her dinner, but she chugged a couple of bottles of Diet Lime Fizzy and barked at the four girls in her charge, "Hurry up! Hurry up!"

She then hurried them to Cabin A to get their shower supplies and toothbrushes and pajamas. She marched them to the showers and stood outside, downing another

Diet Lime Fizzy while she yelled, "Hurry up! Hurry up!" The bathrooms were stinky and moldy. The showers were dank stalls with fat spiders in each corner. Fern had to pull a metal ring on a string to keep the cold water flowing. And flowing might not be the right word. The water was trickling, really. There wasn't enough pressure to get the shampoo out of Fern's hair, so when it dried, it felt somewhat crispy and clumpy. The girls changed quickly into pajamas and brushed their teeth in silence, because Mary Stern kept screaming, "Silence!"

And then Mary Stern put the girls of Cabin A to bed—it was barely light outside. She ordered the girls to be quiet while all of the other campers were just coming back from dinner, singing—those dour marching songs of allegiance were the only songs allowed. These seemed to lend Mary Stern an eerie calm. Her eye had opened back up, and she'd lost her stutter. (Since the most recent attempt on my life—a dart from a dart game that went astray and stabbed the wall behind me as I went to tie my shoe—I've developed a nervous stutter of my own.)

Mary Stern said, "I invented that rule about kicking campers out for good reason, you know. I'm going to enforce that rule. So you'd better be quiet and go to sleep. When I come back to check on you, there'd better be a lot of snoring. Don't you even think about talking. Don't even think of stepping one toe on the floor!" And she slammed out the door.

Fern stared up at the sagging metal underside of the bunk bed above her. Golgatha wasn't a small girl, and Fern imagined the springs busting, the whole contraption falling. She imagined being dissected into a hundred pieces and then smothered by Golgatha and her mattress. It would be an awful way to go. She listened to Mary walk away. And then she promptly got out of bed.

"What are you doing?" Hester whispered. "Are you crazy? You'll get kicked out and then bitten and killed by the Mole and then the Hermit will certainly carry you off and eat you!"

Fern didn't know it was a cannibal hermit. The more she knew about this place, the less she liked it, and she didn't like it at all to begin with! She crouched on the floor now, reaching under Dolores Laverne's cot.

"Get back in bed," Dolores Laverne pleaded. She'd unwound her twisty braids and her hair floated wildly around her face. "She'll know!"

Golgatha was too afraid to say anything. She didn't even turn her head to see what Fern was up to.

"It's okay," Fern said. "I've got something important to do." While she rummaged for the empty bottles, she asked Dolores Laverne how things had been different at camp last year. "Were there mole holes?"

"No," said Dolores Laverne, "there weren't. And Holmquist—"

"Don't answer her, Dolores Laverne," said Hester.

"She's going to get us all in trouble!"

"What about Holmquist? Was he camp director then?"

Dolores Laverne didn't answer. She looked out the screen door and then started to hum anxiously.

Fern had all five of the bottles now. "Please tell me about Holmquist. How was he different? How?"

Dolores Laverne, eyes bugged out, looked at Hester pleadingly, but Hester shook her head no.

"Please tell me," Fern begged. "Please. Maybe I can help get things back to the way they were. Maybe I can help."

Dolores whispered as quickly as possible, "Holmquist lived in a teepee, had a long braid down his back. He taught me what an Anybody truly was. He closed his eyes when he spoke because what he was saying was so wise! And there was no camp director's shiny house. He was, he was . . ."

"What?" Fern asked.

"A guru," Dolores Laverne said. "An Anybody guru. He lived in a simple teepee and he was seen with . . ."

"With? With what? With someone? What happened?" Fern asked.

Dolores Laverne glanced around at Golgatha and Hester, who were shaking their heads, but Dolores Laverne couldn't help it. She blurted out, "The Hermit!"

"No!" Golgatha whispered sharply.

"You shouldn't have told her anything! She'll just make trouble!" Hester scolded.

"No I won't," Fern said. "Tell me more, Dolores Laverne."

But Dolores Laverne put her hand over her mouth and shook her head. She was obviously done.

Fern placed the bottles on her own bunk. It was quiet now. She sat on her bed cross-legged and shook the notes from the bottles. Then she arranged them so that they would make some sense, but she was still thinking about Holmquist in a teepee. What had happened? Why was everything different now? Why had he been with the Hermit, who apparently was so evil?

"What are you doing now?" Hester asked.

"I'm reading," Fern said.

"Well, I don't want to know what you're doing. Don't look, girls," she said to Golgatha and Dolores Laverne.

"I'm already not looking," Dolores Laverne said.

Hester stared at the ceiling and Dolores Laverne stared up at Hester's bunk bed. Golgatha, up above, was too afraid to move an inch. Fern wondered if she was breathing. Fern read to herself.

His name is BORT. He is evil. We are forced to work for him in the basement of some factory. We can hear machines above us and a city above and beyond. Car alarms, a highway.

There's the smell of something burning. It is awful.

We are putting jewels, gems, chandeliers and paintings in boxes to ship to people. Stolen goods.

<u>BORT</u> hates you. He knows you have powers. He talks about you all the time! And we've learned that you are the one who can defeat him.

He wants something from you. He wants to destroy you. But only you can save us.

Well, at least this time there were more clues. A factory. Stolen goods. Something burning. And, most of all, a name. <u>BORT</u>. (Fern didn't yet know that the capitals and underline were intentional, that it was the correct spelling of <u>BORT</u>, as <u>BORT</u> will tell anyone willing to listen. <u>BORT</u> added the underline to his legal name change when he was still a young man.) These things helped, but not much, she had to admit. The facts went around and around in her mind, but there was nothing to grab hold of. She wanted to know what Holmquist had taught Dolores Laverne. She wanted to know what being a true Anybody meant. How could she understand any of this without first knowing that? It was now dark. The air all around Fern was filled with soft snores. Fern took the new Fizzy bottle messages, rolled them up together with the previous ones and secured them with a rubber band.

And then the door swung open. Fern jumped. One of the bottles fell to the floor. It rolled under Dolores Laverne's bunk and bumped against the wall. Dolores Laverne gulped, suddenly wide awake.

Mary Stern was standing there in the doorway. Fern had watched Mary's eyes follow the green bottle under Dolores Laverne's bed.

Fern was scared. Mary Stern radiated a kind of power that some girls can have over other girls. She was a force.

"I can explain," Fern said.

But for once, Mary Stern had very little to say. In fact, she only had one word: "OUT!"

"But I'm only wearing my summer pajamas," said Fern, grabbing hold of the rubber band–wrapped messages and her backpack.

Mary Stern's chin was held high. Her eyes were closed in disgust. She pointed her finger into the night, and Fern had no choice but to go out into it.

KICKED OUT

THE FULL MOON CAST STRANGE SHADOWS. TREE knots looked like eyes, sticks like snakes. The crickets were screeching. The forest was filled with rustling noises that Fern imagined to be racoons and mice and owls and bats—a vicious mole, a hermit who wanted to eat her up? The forest seemed more alive than it did during the day. In fact, Fern felt like the small breeze that sometimes slipped from the line of trees was an exhale. The forest seemed to be breathing.

Fern didn't have a flashlight. She was holding on to her roll of bottle messages tightly. She walked carefully, trying to avoid the bare roots and mole holes. (Speaking of mole holes, did I mention that I recently slipped down a manhole? Luckily I survived. A fairly heavy woman had fallen in just before me. No one had noticed, but when I fell, I landed on her—a soft cushion. And I only landed partially on my head, which, it turns out, is quite rubbery. It was a defective manhole, so I was told. But I know who was behind it!) Fern needed to find Howard. Maybe he'd be able to sneak her into his cabin for the night. In any case, it would be nice to see a familiar face. Unfortunately she didn't know what cabin he was assigned to. Maybe this was on purpose. And so she went first to Boys' Cabin A. She found a window and she whispered, "Howard? Howard?"

"No Howard here," a small voice responded from the dark.

"Sorry, thank you."

"You're quite welcome!"

Fern went to Boys' Cabin B and found a window. "Howard? Are you in there? Howard?"

There was no answer, so she cupped her hands to the screen and tried to peer inside. "Howard?" she said a little louder.

But then a counselor with a large badger snout shot up to the frame. "What do you want? Who are you? Get back to your cabin!"

Fern was so scared that she stumbled backward,

tripping over a mole hole, but quickly jumped up and started running.

When she got to Boys' Cabin C, she was breathless and shaking. *Please be here, Howard*, she thought in her head. *Please!* She whispered very softly. "Howard? Is this your cabin? Howard?"

And this time another face popped up—the pale, round face of Howard himself!

"Thank goodness!" Fern gushed. "I sure am happy to see you!"

Howard gave a genuine smile. It was the first genuine

smile she'd seen on him in a while. Maybe ever? Could it be that he was happy to see her, too? But he didn't say so. "Everything's gone wrong!" he whispered.

"I thought you loved it here," Fern said.

"I was faking it. That Corky Gorsky is bad news, Fern. That's what I'm telling you!"

"But you love him?"

"I do not!"

"You hugged him!"

"I had to! He hypnotized me, Fern. Well, he tried to, but I resisted. I kept digging my fingernails into my palms to stay alert and I faked the trance."

All of this was very comforting news to Fern. Howard wasn't crazy enough to love it here. He was smart, doing the best he could. But was there really something wrong with Corky Gorsky? "Where is he now?"

"He's not here! He took off after our counselor left. He said he had to go to the bathroom. But it's been over an hour. He could be anywhere. Look, Fern, he's trouble. For some reason, he's desperate that we like him."

"Well, maybe he just wants friends!" Fern said, reminding herself why she'd wanted to come to camp and how she hadn't really done so well in the friend department.

"Trust me! There's something wrong with Corky Gorsky." There was a quiet moment. A little pause. And then Howard said, "Hey, what are you doing at my window in the middle of the night?"

"I got kicked out."

"Oh." This didn't surprise him. "What are you going to do?"

"I thought I'd maybe come into your cabin . . . ?"

"No way. I'm supposed to be hypnotized to love it here, everything about it here, including the rules. Actually, that's the one part of this whole thing that I like. I need to follow the rules, Fern. It seems like ever since I met you, I've been mangling rules left and right. And I want to be a rule follower. I don't want to get into any more trouble. Look, I'll keep trying to figure out what Corky's up to . . . exactly. You'll just have to tough it out."

"Tough it out?" Fern said. Did toughing it out include getting attacked by a mole and devoured by a hermit?

"Yep! Tough it out."

And with that Howard's moonish face disappeared.

"Howard?"

"No. Go away."

"Howard, please."

"Do I have to call my counselor?"

"Okay, okay," Fern said. "Calm down. But listen to me, if you hear anything about a guy named BORT, you let me know."

Howard reappeared. "BORT?"

"Yes, BORT," she said. "And take these." She handed Howard the rolled-up Fizzy bottle messages, now damp from being held so tightly in her sweaty fist.

"Okay," Howard said, taking the roll. And, with that, he disappeared again.

As Fern walked away from Boys' Cabin C, she was furious with Howard. She was mocking him under her breath, *"Tough it out. Tough it out."* How dare he suggest toughing it out when he was safe and secure in his cabin and she had to survive the night in the forest! (This is the kind of thing that I sometimes think when I'm in a difficult situation. And these days, I'm often in difficult situations. Word to the wise: if a free pass to play golf shows up in your mailbox on a cloudy day, and if you decide to play golf, and if a stranger offers you an umbrella with an extra-tall metal tip on top of it during a thunderstorm on this golf course, decline the umbrella. Say, "No thank you. Although that's very kind, I must be going now." Then run to your car.)

It was dark, and the forest was breathing again. Fern wasn't sure what she was going to do. She was wondering how she would ever find the Nobodies and how she'd be able to help them if she did. She was wondering if Howard was right that there was something wrong with Corky Gorsky. Where was he? Was he out here in the forest somewhere? Maybe he was just a kid who asked a lot of questions because he never really knew what to say. Maybe he'd hypnotized Howard because he really wanted Howard to like him. Fern wanted to be liked too, and Mary Stern hated her, and the other girls were too afraid to try to be friends with her. She felt helpless and small and defenseless. She wanted a friend. A real friend. Not Howard, who wanted to follow every rule, who wanted to be in a living room somewhere discussing weed killer, who wanted to be extremely normal! She wanted a real friend who was just like she was!

She was thinking that things couldn't get much worse than this, but she was wrong. They could. In fact, they did. She heard some distant hooting, the loose call of an owl. Another owl responded. Then there was another bird cry that Fern couldn't make out. The calls grew louder from deep in the forest. Fern saw one of the cabin doors open. A counselor peeked his head out. He looked somewhat skunky, a white stripe running through his black hair. Then Claussen Peevish's sharp beak poked out of the door of the Boy Counselors' Cabin. The two boys nodded to each other. A few girl counselors stepped out of the Girl Counselors' Cabin, Mary Stern among them. They looked up at the night sky, as if searching out the birds. Fern looked up too. The sky was clear. The girls looked scared. One started crying, but Mary

Stern and the others pulled her along.

"We have to!" she heard one say. "We have no choice!"

Claussen and the skunk boy had already headed into the forest. The girls followed. Fern stood there, frozen. She didn't want to go into the forest, especially since that one girl was so terrified, but she didn't want to be alone, either. After a minute she took the trail that the girls had disappeared into. The trail ran alongside of the frothy, stinky pond. Big birds screeched right overhead. Fern could hear the heavy thudding of big wings. There were owls, yes, but also vultures, buzzards. One large bird careened through the trees and then another. She watched their brown and gray bodies lift from tree to tree. Fern looked up into the trees, and she could make out in the moonlight their soft pink, human feet with long, clawed toenails. They were boys, Fern realized. She looked at one of them and could make out the eyes of Claussen Peevish.

Now Fern could smell the sharp rising stink of a skunk. She caught sight of a white tail slipping into the underbrush. She stood there quite still. Was it just a coincidence? The skunk boy and the real skunk here now? Fern walked over to the underbrush. She balanced along a hollow log. Then she spotted the skunk again by the edge of the murky pond. She stepped toward it. The skunk heard her coming. It reared and hissed. Fern could make out its human nose, its human lips.

"Are you a counselor?" she asked.

For a moment it seemed like the skunk might answer. It cocked its head, glanced around and leaned forward as if about to tell a secret. But then the skunk turned on her and sprayed. Fern was caught in a deathly awful, stinking fog. Her eyes streamed with tears, and her nose was running. She coughed and gagged. When she looked up to find the skunk, it was gone. But the wretched scent wasn't. It clung to Fern. Her heart was pounding in her chest. What was happening here? She staggered a few steps into the pond, trying to wipe the stench from her clothes, her arms, her hair. The giant birds were screeching again. Were they circling her? Were they hunting her? They seemed to be eyeing her, gliding overhead. Was Corky out here somewhere? Fern wondered. "Corky?" she whispered through a hacking cough. She walked backward, away from them, but the large flapping birds kept coming closer, lighting down on lower and lower branches. Claussen Peevish was among them.

"Claussen!" she yelled out. "I know it's you!"

And now another giant bird, a sleek white one with a large beak, screeched and leaped off his branch. Aiming for Fern's heart, he lifted his clawed feet as he glided toward her. But then Claussen appeared, and he clawed the white bird before it had a chance to claw Fern. The two large birds rustled on the ground ferociously. They clawed and pecked each other on the muddy bank. Plumage gusted up from their beating wings. Fern backed deeper into the pond. Her feet sank into the silt. Claussen had saved her.

"Claussen!" she yelled. "Claussen!"

The white bird was now dotted with blood; Claussen, too, though it was harder to make out.

Just then she heard a great rushing noise behind her. She turned. And there, rising up, was the scaley, pointed face of Mary Stern, a slick fish arching up in the water. The birds from the pond flew off in a mad rustling of wings. And Mary Stern said in a thick, watery whisper, "Go, Fern. It's not safe here. Go!" And then it seemed Mary Stern was jerked back into the pond, and all that was left was a circle of rings on the water's surface.

NURSE HURLEY

FERN RAN, STUMBLING OVER ROOTS AND MOLE holes, falling, bruising her knees, getting up and running again. She ran as fast as she could back to the cabins, her backpack with all three books bouncing heavily on her back. She stood, panting, in the middle of the circle near the charred wood of the bonfire. Her eyes darted from cabin to cabin. Where could she go?

Fern knew that her foul skunk smell was strong when Gus Watershed's large head popped out of a window in his small cabin. He raised his nose in the air, took offense and slammed all his windows shut.

After he disappeared and it seemed that no one else

was near, Fern couldn't shake the feeling of being watched. (I'm always being watched as well, so I can surely sympathize with Fern.) Where was Corky Gorsky? she kept wondering. Was he out here somewhere, watching her? She peered into the moonlit trees, looking for more strange creatures, especially the white bird. Was this what it could be like to be an Anybody? For her grandmother, it had been good to be a blue butterfly doing the right thing in the world, hadn't it? But could it also be this awful, horrifying transformation, this danger that Mary Stern, the bright, moonlit fish, had just warned her about? And why had Mary Stern warned her? Didn't she hate her? Why had the awful Claussen Peevish saved her? It made no sense.

Fern, still staring into the trees, could make out one shifting shape. A ghost in the trees? A billowing skirt? No, a dog, the stray Seeing Eye dog, white with one brown-spotted ear. The dog, bounding this way and that. Did she want Fern to follow her? She was dodging in and out of the trees. Fern couldn't follow her. She felt awful. Dizzy. Trapped in the putrid mist of the skunk.

And then it hit her—the nurse's cabin with its red cross. She ran to it and opened the door. This cabin smelled like wet socks, but also peroxide and ointments and tongue depressors, Band-Aids and now skunk. There in the glow of a small night-light, she could make out a lump, snoring in an easy chair, a paunchy woman in a white nurse's uniform and thick, white stockings. There were only two doors in the small cabin. Fern opened one—a bathroom—and then the next—another small room. It had a cot. Fern wanted to slip into its stiff, starched sheets. But just then the nurse started snorting and coughing.

"What? What is that—that—that. . . ," she sputtered. "What is that smell?" She popped the lever on her old La-Z-Boy and, in one flumping motion, was jettisoned to her feet. "Dear heavens, who's run into the wrong end of a skunk?"

"I have," Fern said, stepping into some moonlight.

The nurse stared at Fern. She stumbled backward. She said, "Is it . . . is it? Am I dreaming still?" She walked up to Fern and held out her arm. "Pinch me! Go ahead and pinch!"

Fern pinched the nurse's jubby arm.

"Ouch! That hurt!"

"You told me to," Fern said.

"I thought I was dreaming. I thought you were another little girl I once knew. A girl who once came in here smelling just like you do at this very moment."

"Who was that?"

"Her name was Eliza, but that was years and years ago. Sometimes when I'm dreaming, I lose track of time.

151

Sometimes when I'm awake, too. Time is always changing, though. It's a swirling state of being we live in, isn't it?" She looked sharply at Fern. "Who are you?"

"My mother's name was Eliza. I'm Fern. Her daughter."

"Dorathea's granddaughter?"

"Yes."

"Well, of course you are! I knew it! I knew it! I'm Nurse Hurley," she said, sticking out her hand to shake Fern's, but then, still aware of the skunk stink, gave a little wave instead. "You don't mind, but I'd rather not. . . ."

"It's okay," Fern said. "Will the stink come off?"

"Oh, no. It won't."

"It won't?" Fern felt a sharp panic. Would she stink for the rest of her life?

"No, of course not. The stink will transform!" Nurse Hurley said, running her thumb over the book bindings on her shelves—*Healing Through Hypnosis* and *Turning Itch into Tickle: Easy Allergy Remedies.*

"Oh," Fern said, relieved. "What will it transform into?"

"Why, another smell, of course. Unless you want it to transform into a wart."

"No, thanks," Fern said. "Another smell will be fine." She pulled a book off the shelf—*The Flux of Scent: An*

Ever-Changing Property—and started flipping pages. Fern wondered what was inside all these books. Could hypnosis really heal someone? Could it have healed her mother in the hospital giving birth? Could it have saved her life?

"What are all these books about?" Fern asked Nurse Hurley.

"Medical texts. Anybody cures."

"Do they work?"

"They help," Nurse Hurley said.

"Are there Anybody doctors?" Fern asked.

"Of course. In fact, some truly great Anybodies with much experience can quite often cure themselves."

"My mother couldn't save herself," Fern said.

"No, a sad day for us all," Nurse Hurley said softly. "When it's your time to go, it's your time. It's beyond your control. Being an Anybody doctor is an imperfect science. The properties of being an Anybody are always changing, right? As is life. You know the old tried-and-true Anybody philosophies."

"No," Fern said. "What philosophies?"

Nurse Hurley looked up from her book. She snapped it shut angrily. A pop of dust rose up around it. She slammed it down on a table and started pacing. She walked over to the window and looked at Holmquist's deluxe house. "It's those two!" she said.

153

"What are they doing, anyhow? What have they let this place become?"

"I don't know," Fern said, her eyes still stinging from her own stink.

"Well, they're ruining this camp. I can tell you that. Letting those counselors be in charge of everything. And what's the result? That varmint on the loose! Children out on the loose at night being sprayed by skunks. And nobody being taught anything, not anything. "

"It's only my first day," Fern said.

"Yes, yes, but still! I heard you all repeating that silly oath and not a thing was said about the true calling! Not a thing about the world being in a constant state of change." She walked over to Fern, bent down and said, "Listen. Being an Anybody is being in tune with the world's chaos and constant flux. True Anybodies know that nothing is fixed, still, stationary. Being an Anybody is a normal way of living for those in touch with the world's natural state. Does that make sense?"

"A little," Fern said.

"An Anybody is someone who's gained an advantage—through evolution. By accepting the world's constant change, we can change, transform. We can use this advantage for good—like me, as a nurse. Or for self gain, like countless Anybodies who have joined the general population so that they can get ahead. Or for the pure calling of art. Or . . ." She trailed off. She walked to the window again, peering into the darkness.

Fern's mind flashed back to the skunk's human eyes, the pink human feet of the enormous birds, Claussen Peevish fighting the white one, and Mary Stern rearing up as a giant fish—Mary Stern, who had never before spoken to her so kindly. "Or?" Fern asked.

"Or for evil," Nurse Hurley said. "Pure evil."

Fern wanted to know if she was looking at Holmquist's deluxe house or not. Was Holmquist evil? She fiddled nervously with the straps of her backpack. "Who uses it for evil?" Fern asked. "Holmquist?"

"Ha! Holmquist. No, not Holmquist, but watch out for his mother. That's all I can tell you. Auggie Holmquist. She's not a good egg," Nurse Hurley said. "Not at all."

"Why?" Fern asked. "Why isn't she a good egg?" Her name sounded familiar to Fern somehow. Had she heard of Auggie Holmquist before?

"Well, Holmquist was doing just fine before Auggie came back into his life! The kids here used to be so wise when they left. But this summer, here she shows up and everything's a mess! But let's not dwell. No, no," Nurse Hurley said. "We've got work to do. You smell awful."

Nurse Hurley went to a cupboard, pulled out three enormous cans of tomato soup, and heaved them one by one into the bathroom. She pierced the lids with a can opener from her Swiss Army knife and glugged them into the tub.

"That's what everyone does for skunk stink," Fern said. "Isn't it? I mean it's an old wives' tale—tomato soup baths for skunk. Right?" The tub was filling with thick red soup. The room already filled with skunk stink now smelled like tomato-skunk stew.

"Yes," Nurse Hurley said, dripping the last bit of soup into the tub. "Yes, it is the normal remedy. Except for one thing."

"What?"

"If you don't want to smell like skunk, what would you want to smell like?"

Fern thought for a moment, but it was only the briefest moment. She knew exactly what she wanted to smell like—her mother. And her mother always smelled like one thing—lilacs. "Lilacs," Fern said.

And Nurse Hurley looked up at her. "Yes," she said. "I remember that now. Eliza and her lilacs."

Nurse Hurley took out a pocket watch on a long gold chain. She swung it above the tub of soup. She hummed, a steady hum that seemed to rev in her chest. The tub of tomato soup continued to look like a tub of tomato soup, but slowly the tomato soup stink gave way to something buttery, then something sugary, then a light tangy fruit with sunshine pouring down on it, and finally a sweeping tide of the scent of lilacs—a whole wild, bushy field of them.

"I'll leave you now so you can take a good long soak," Nurse Hurley said. "Don't forget to wash behind your ears."

Fern stood there for a moment, staring into the red tub. She rubbed her bruised knees and then closed her eyes and drank in the smell of lilacs, the smell of her mother. She took off her backpack, and then her paja-mas, folding them up. She stuck her toe in the soup. It was warm. She stepped into the tub, lay down and let herself relax, the soup up to her chin. The lilac smell was heavy and sweet, so sweet it almost made Fern start to cry. For a moment she felt taken care of, protected. She felt like her mother was right there with her. She closed her eyes.

But then her mind flashed to Claussen Peevish

thrashing and bleeding. Hadn't he been trying to save her? And Mary Stern, too, with her watery warning? What was happening here? Fern had a feeling that the counselors were in grave danger. Did they spend their nights trapped in the bodies of animals? *Why,* Fern asked herself. *How?* All her answers, half-formed, jumbled, confused, led back to one name: the Mole.

CLAUSSEN PEEVISH—STRICKEN!

THE NEXT MORNING FERN WOKE UP IN THE COT
in Nurse Hurley's cabin. Through the open door of the
room, Fern could see that Nurse Hurley was still sleeping in the La-Z-Boy recliner. The sunlight shone on her
puffed face. Her mouth was open, and there was a thin
trail of spit suspended like a tightrope from bottom lip
to top. Fern didn't want to disturb her. She tiptoed past.

Nurse Hurley had given her a pair of shorts and a
baggy T-shirt to change into the night before. Nurse
Hurley said she'd wash her summer pajamas for her
and return them. Fern didn't let her take the backpack,
though. She needed to keep that with her. And so now

159

she swung it on one shoulder. It smelled like a sickly mixture of faded skunk and lilacs.

Fern slipped out quietly and started to jog back to her cabin. There were kids already in the mess tent, clattering trays. The kids cutting across the bonfire circle whispered to one another feverishly. No one was singing those awful marching songs of allegiance. In fact, everyone was being very, very quiet, engrossed in hushed conversations.

Because Fern was watching the clumps of whisperers and not where she was going, she ran smack into Golgatha, Dolores Laverne and Hester. They tumbled backward like a small set of dominoes. Mary Stern had been yelling at them to hurry up from the back of the line. She was hit hardest. She fell down, her rump skidding twice on the hard dirt. She spilled some of her Diet Lime Fizzy on the front of her counselor shirt. She wasn't fishy, as she'd been the night before. There were only the small gill holes flapping on her neck, barely noticeable, as they'd been yesterday. But where was the Mary Stern who had risen up from the murky pond to warn Fern? Would Mary Stern mention it? Would she even remember it?

"Fern! Look what you did!" Mary Stern pointed to her shirt, as if Fern needed help figuring it out. "Running around, pushing and shoving, all against the rules! You've just earned another night kicked out of your cabin! My, my, and all before breakfast! You're quite a wonder!"

"I didn't mean to," Fern said.

"I don't care! You shouldn't be acting so wild! Don't you know we've had an incident! Claussen Peevish. Poor Claussen. He's in Holmquist's office at this very moment." Mary Stern pointed to the lovely air-conditioned house sitting back in the trees. Fern noticed a bandage on her pinky—bulky white gauze wrapped with tape. "His parents are going to have to come and get him."

"What happened to Claussen?" Fern asked.

"Don't ask!" said Dolores Laverne, her braids so tight-wound that her eyelids were taut. Two tears popped out of her eyes.

"It's awful," said Golgatha.

"He should have been more careful!" said Hester.

"What happened?" Fern asked again.

And Mary Stern said, "Claussen Peevish got in a fight with another boy. He picked the fight. He wasn't thinking clearly. He should have minded his own business. And then he got attacked by the Mole."

"The Mole?"

"What's that smell?" Mary Stern asked. "Fern, are you wearing perfume?"

"No," Fern said. "I mean yes. I don't know!" She pointed to Mary Stern's hand. "What happened to your pinky?"

"Nothing."

"Did you show it to Nurse Hurley?"

"No. No one needs to go to Hurley. She doesn't know anything! Claussen should have followed the rules, that's all!"

"What rules?" Fern asked.

"The rules, Fern." And then she blinked and stared at Fern in an odd way, as if she were suddenly very frightened. It was the same expression as when she was a fish, warning Fern the night before. "Oh, Fern!" she said. "Oh, the rules . . ." And she hid her face in her hands. Was she crying? Was Mary Stern crying?

Dolores Laverne patted her gently on the back. "It's okay," she said.

But then Mary Stern snapped out of it. "Of course it's okay! Rules are rules." She finished what was left of her soda and handed the bottle to Fern. "Throw this away. Get dressed. And be in the mess tent. Pronto!"

Fern jogged back to her cabin. All her things were lumped on her bunk. They'd been rummaged through. Her clothes, her toiletries. It was lucky she'd taken all her Fizzy bottle messages with her and given them to Howard.

She wasn't too surprised that someone had gone through her things. Mary Stern might have been looking for evidence to get her kicked out for good. Or, worse, the Mole was looking for *The Art of Being Anybody*.

In either case, they hadn't found anything except sweat socks and ponytail holders. Fern had *The Art of Being Anybody*, her mother's diary and her own diary safe in her backpack, with her now at all times.

Fern hurriedly got dressed. She wanted desperately to write down everything that had happened in her journal. She dug her diary out of her backpack and began to unlock her diary with the key she wore as a necklace, just to jot a note or two. But as soon as the lock clicked open, Diet Lime Fizzy bottles came pouring out. They clunked onto the uneven floorboards and rolled and rolled and rolled, piling up under Dolores Laverne's bunk. Fern tried to shut the diary. She squeezed its covers together with all her might. She forced it to the ground and sat on it. Finally it shut, and Fern locked it. She put the book down on her bed, but it rattled and quivered with bottles still trying to burst out.

Bottles! All those bottles stuffed with notes! Fern wanted to ignore them. She already had a lot to deal with. A vicious mole on the loose. A counselor who hated her . . . or did she? Those night creatures. Not to mention Corky Gorsky, who was or was not a bad guy. Had he too been out in the forest the night before? And Howard, who'd abandoned her to the woods. She was trying to survive as best she could. How could she possibly save anyone else? She concentrated on getting dressed. The bottles were already nicely hidden under

Dolores Laverne's bunk. Maybe they could just sit there and collect dust until Fern was ready to deal with them.

But, no. Fern could still smell the lilac in her hair and on her skin. She remembered the dream of her mother and what her mother had said to her: "*You have to save them, Fern. I can't, but you can, my dear. You can.*" Fern knelt down, picked up a bottle and shook the note out onto the floor. This one was much different than the others. First of all, it was a mess. It started out fine enough, but then got mushed up in that way that kids write when they run out of room. Actually, it was very, very much like the signs written to label things at camp!

Fern, I'm the one who told all the Nobodies about you. Someone once told me how famous you are. I'm not a Nobody, but I am a nobody, if you know what I mean. I used to have a fine job, but BORT hauled me off and has left me here. You can save us. I have faith in you. Sincerely, Mickey

Mickey? Who was Mickey? The letter was meant to inspire Fern, but it only made her feel hot and sweaty and useless. She shoved the note into her pocket and quickly dumped all the other notes out of the bottles. There wasn't enough time to read them. She shoved them, one by one, into her pockets until they bulged. When the last one was tucked away, Fern's cabin door swung open. There was Howard and, beside him, standing there, normal as ever in his Band-Aid–covered nose, was, yep, you guessed it, Corky Gorsky.

"Hey, guess what?" Corky said. "Since Claussen Peevish got attacked last night, our group is going to pair up with your group today. So we'll get to spend more time together after all."

"Isn't that great!" exclaimed Howard, a hysterical squeak in his voice, eyes bulging, the force of his smile jiggling his cheeks.

"Great!" echoed Fern with fake zeal. "Great, great!"

CANCELLATION, MEMORIZATION AND ASSIMILATION

THE CLOSEST FERN COULD COME TO GOOD NEWS was that Dolores Laverne, in an act of kindness, had stolen a plastic spoon and a paper cup full of oatmeal from the mess tent for Fern's breakfast. It had gone cold and lumpy, but Fern was thankful that Dolores Laverne had been thinking of her. Fern ate the oatmeal in her cabin, hiding in the back of the packed-in clump of campers—those from her tribe and the boys from Boys' Cabin C, who were all together now.

The bad news, on the other hand, was overflowing. There were Diet Lime Fizzy bottles, all filled with desperate messages, ready to pour out of her diary. The Mole, who'd viciously attacked Claussen Peevish, was on the loose. Mary Stern had kicked her out of her cabin again for the upcoming night. She was beginning to wonder if she would ever get to sleep in her bunk. She and Howard were going to be in the same group of campers with Corky Gorsky. And Mary Stern, taking the lead now that Claussen was gone, was announcing through her wire braces, her neck gills flapping, that all regular camp activities would be canceled.

"With the Mole out there hunting for us, we have to take every precaution! The boys of Cabin C and the girls of Cabin A, under my direction, will be staying indoors, memorizing the *Camp Happy Sunshine Good Times Handbook.*"

Howard was the only one who looked happy. *Memorizing a handbook,* Fern thought, *is just the kind of thing that Howard would choose to do for fun.*

"Does this mean we won't be learning any Anybody skills?" asked Marshall, a scrawny camper from Boys' Cabin C who had a fluffy puff of black hair. His twin brother, Maxwell, was sitting beside him. They were very hard to tell apart, but Fern decided that Maxwell's hair was more airy and roomy than Marshall's, and so she could just barely keep them straight.

"That's correct," Mary Stern said.

167

Fern felt a flush of anguish. She wasn't going to learn anything? But she'd wanted to know what a true Anybody was. That's what Holmquist had taught Dolores Laverne the year before. That's what Fern was dying to understand, really understand, about herself and this group of people, her people.

"What were we going to learn?" asked Hester, quite bravely.

"I cannot impart that information!" Mary Stern said sharply, sipping from a Fizzy bottle. "Sit down." And so the campers quickly sat down on the cabin floor, legs crisscrossed.

"If we have to stay indoors, does that mean that my punishment is canceled too? Am I going to be able to sleep in the cabin tonight?" Fern asked hopefully.

"No. A punishment is a punishment!" Mary Stern answered, passing out handbooks. "Begin on page one. The table of contents. I expect this to be memorized with corresponding page numbers by lunch."

The group sighed dejectedly, except for Howard and Corky Gorsky, who wrapped one arm around Fern and one arm around Howard with a spirit of camaraderie. "We can do it!" he said cheerfully. "Can't we?"

"That's the spirit," Mary Stern said sourly. "Now get to work!"

The only nice thing about the whole scenario was that

Mary Stern became bored quickly, and she wandered to sit on a bunk by a window. She shook candies out of a special order catalogue, washing them down with gulps of Diet Lime Fizzy. Then she shook one loud pop song after another out of her *Teen Idol* magazine. Despite herself, Fern was impressed. It hadn't ever dawned on her to shake candies out of a catalogue. Was that a form of stealing? Nor had she ever imagine shaking music from a book. But of course! She'd once shaken her mother's lilac perfume from her mother's diary. It had been one of her greatest comforts. If you could shake out a smell, why not music? Mary Stern sang along off-key, crunching and guzzling while staring out the window at the murky pond.

"Introduction," Corky said, "page four. That's easy enough to remember! You got that, Howard?"

"Got it," Howard said, his nose in his handbook.

"This is a waste of time," Fern said.

"Maybe," said Corky, "but at least we're wasting time together. It could be worse. Haven't you experienced worse?"

Fern looked at Corky. "Why do you always ask questions?"

"What's in your backpack?"

"That doesn't even make sense! Why would you ask about my backpack now? I'm not telling you!"

"Why not?"

"Stop asking questions," Fern said, trying to keep her voice down so Mary Stern wouldn't hear it over her pop songs. "Why do you keep doing that? Answer me!"

Corky paused a minute. It was obviously harder for him to answer questions than to ask them. "Um. It's good to ask questions," Corky said nervously. "You're supposed to, if you want to find things out."

"What do you want to find out?"

"Nothing," Corky said. "Nothing! What do you want to find out?"

"Stop it! Stop asking questions. Can't you tell we've stopped answering them?"

Corky looked very upset now. "You have?"

"We stopped answering a long time ago," Fern told him.

"You too, Howard? You've stopped answering my questions?"

Howard was quiet. He was afraid of Corky. He didn't want to say anything to give the impression that he wasn't under Corky's control. So he just smiled stupidly and shook his head and then nodded it and then shrugged and put his face back in the handbook, his eyes gliding across the pages.

"Howard," Fern said. "Why don't you ask Corky a question, huh? Why don't you try that?"

CANCELLATION, MEMORIZATION AND ASSIMILATION

"No, no," Corky said. "That's okay."

"But how else is Howard going to find things out about you, Corky Gorsky? How will he ever really know the real Corky Gorsky?"

"No, not necessary. That's okay. Shouldn't we be studying the handbook?"

Fern glared at Howard, who refused to look up. She looked at Corky. "I've got a question: where were you last night? You went to the bathroom and then you were gone for hours. Can you explain that?"

Corky shook his head. "I got lost!"

"Really! Huh! That surprises me, because I was out there all night and I didn't run into you once. Or did I?"

"What's that supposed to mean?" Corky asked defensively.

"I think you might know what it means!"

Corky was getting angry now. His face was red. "I don't know what you mean, Fern!"

"Well, finally, you've stopped asking questions!"

"Hey, hey," Howard broke in, "why can't we all get along here? Camp's about being friends!" He looked at Fern nervously.

"I'm going over to memorize the handbook with Dolores Laverne," Fern said.

Corky looked at her sadly all of a sudden. He

171

shrugged. "Do whatever you want to, Fern."

Fern walked past Hester and Golgatha huddled on Hester's bunk. Their eyes snapped up from their handbooks. Fern smiled. They didn't smile back. Fern walked on to Dolores Laverne, who was sitting alone on her bottom bunk. Her braids were bundled so thickly on top of her head that she looked like a swami. A small, frightened, mousy swami.

"Hi, Dolores Laverne," Fern said.

"Shhh!" Dolores Laverne hissed without looking up.

Fern lowered her voice. "I thought maybe we could study together."

"No, you didn't," she said, glancing at Hester and Golgatha, who were gawking. Hester shook her head, meaning *Don't talk to Fern!* Golgatha scowled.

"I didn't?"

"No. You want information out of me."

Dolores Laverne was right. Fern wanted to hear about what she was missing. What kind of Anybody lessons had Dolores Laverne learned last summer? Fern wanted to hear more about Holmquist and what he'd said when he was a guru in a teepee. But she decided to play it cool. She didn't want to scare Dolores Laverne off. "Nah," she said. "I just wanted to get away from the boys."

"Boys!" Dolores Laverne huffed. "I have four brothers. Don't even talk to me about boys!" She kept glanc-

ing at Hester and Golgatha, but the two had given up
on her with a demoralized shrug. They had memorizing
to do, and they were going at it at a feverish pace,
mumbling rhythmically and flipping pages.

"Yeah," Fern agreed. "Boys! Are your brothers at
camp?"

"Not this year, thank goodness." Just then Mary Stern
shifted in her seat and swiveled around, eyeing everyone
coldly. When she turned back to her catalogues, Dolores
Laverne went on in a hurried whisper. "They're all older.
They went here for years, though. They're really good
Anybodies. And now I won't learn anything! My parents
are members of AWP. Not artsy types."

"What's AWP?"

"Anybodies with Purpose. They believe in using their
abilities to get ahead. My mother is gorgeous. She's a
motivational speaker. And my father runs a bank, you
know, for ice cubes."

"Ice cubes?"

"Don't you know anything? That's slang. Ice cubes
are, you know, non-Anybodies. You know, they can't
transform. They're frozen in their shapes. They're ice
cubes."

"Oh," Fern said. "I get it."

"They say it's like melting, you know. When you
move into another form. My brothers told me."

That sounded wonderful to Fern. She wanted to know what it would feel like to melt into a different shape. She'd seen a nun turn into a lamppost, a bird turn into a dog, a man turn into a bull, a butterfly turn into a mouse. She'd even seen her father pop out of an ordinary record player. But she'd never learned how to transform into anything. She'd taken her grandmother's instructions seriously and had always gone through *The Art of Being Anybody* step by mastered step, waiting for the right moment. But would it ever come?

Dolores Laverne continued, "Every morning my mom melts into a younger face, white teeth, blond hair. And my dad smooths people at work. You know, a little hypnosis, gentle action, to get ahead. They're all for assimilation into the general public and, you know, pro-AWP. What are your parents?"

"My mother's dead," Fern said. It was the first time she'd ever had to tell anyone. She'd been the last to know, and so there was no one else to tell. It surprised her that it came out so easily but stung so sharply in her chest. "I don't know what my dad and grandmother are."

"Do they live isolated? Or do they use their powers to get ahead? Do they believe being an Anybody is an art?"

"They live pretty far out of town. And I think they do see it as an art. Yes, my dad said that once." He'd said it when he'd first described being an Anybody to Fern.

"Really?" Dolores Laverne looked shocked. "They do? That's amazing."

"Is it?"

"Well, I think it's amazing. I've always wanted to be an artistic Anybody. Holmquist used to teach it that way—being an Anybody is a calling. He'd say being an Anybody is knowing that the world is—"

"Always changing," Fern said.

"Right! The fact that we can take a book and shake something real from it, well, the writer's already done the work for all of us. It's Anybodies who not only feel the world that's being written, but can shake it, transform it into being. Paintings and music, too." She nodded toward Mary Stern. "It's just another type of transforming, the imagined into the real. He told us that we're the chameleons, the pollywogs, the monarch butterflies of the human world."

"That's beautiful," Fern said.

"Well, I'm not a natural, so I just went to the lessons and listened and tried to shake things and to transform, to melt, but nothing happened. I'm not good at melting."

"I'm sure with some practice you'd be really good."

"Well, I'm not going to get any practice here, am I?"

At that moment Mary Stern jumped up. "What was that? Did you hear that?" She picked up her *Teen Idol* magazine and swept it through the air like a net, getting all the noisy music back into its pages. The cabin fell silent. No one said a word. Mary Stern leaned out the window. An owl hooted loudly overhead. "No, no," Mary Stern said. "It can't. It's daytime. The sun is clearly up. No!"

Mary Stern started to shake. She grabbed her candies and her magazine and her catalogue and dropped them into a canvas bag with the words "Camp Happy Sunshine Good Times" printed on it in blue letters. "No, no, no," she was muttering to herself, and then she turned around, as if suddenly remembering the campers. They stared at her, and she stared back. "I have to go!" she said. "I've got . . . um . . . important business. Just stay here, will you? Stay here; keep memorizing!"

"What is it?" Fern asked.

"Mind your own beeswax!" Mary Stern said.

"Aren't you going to quiz us on the handbooks?" Howard asked, obviously desiring some praise for his hard work.

"I'll be back!" said Mary Stern. "And when I'm back, this whole handbook has to be memorized, or else!"

Fern wanted to ask, *Or else what?* But didn't. Mary

Stern didn't look right. She was saying all of the normal mean things, but her voice was shaky. She looked upset. Something was very wrong. Fern was sure that they were all in danger—Mary Stern, the other counselors, the campers too. Fern wanted to go with Mary Stern, but she knew she wouldn't be allowed. She watched Mary Stern swing her bag over her shoulder and storm out of the cabin, the door crashing behind her.

And for a long, sickening moment, everything was quiet. Then there was one piercing noise, and then another, and then a chorus. Fern knew what it was. Through the open window, off in the distance, coming out of the forest, echoed the awful howling of vultures and buzzards and owls.

INTO THE WOODS

THIS LEFT THE EIGHT OF THEM—FOUR GIRLS AND
four boys. Fern looked around. Marshall and Maxwell
sat there, staring out from their matching sets of wide
eyes. Golgatha grabbed hold of Hester, and Dolores
Laverne pulled her lips into a nervous little thin line.
Howard was still smiling, a plastered-on kind of smile,
but he was sweating, too. Corky Gorsky was looking
at Fern. And Fern was now looking straight at Corky
Gorsky. She could feel her stomach knot.

"I think. . . ," Fern began. "I think—"

"I agree," Corky interrupted.

"But I didn't even finish!"

"But I knew what you were going to say," Corky said.

"Maybe I was going to say that I think we should all eat lizard tongues? Or that we should braid Dolores Laverne's hair straight up on top of her head?"

Dolores Laverne shook her head, "No, no thanks," she said nervously.

"Or . . . or—," Fern tried to go on.

"Look, this is it! It's go time," interrupted Corky. "We should follow Mary Stern. Something's up, and we should find out what it is. It's a good idea."

This was exactly what Fern was going to say. It felt odd that she and Corky seemed suddenly to be on the same team. It made her nervous. She still didn't trust Corky.

"But only you and I should go, Fern."

"Why not the whole group?" she asked.

Corky turned around and, with a wave of his hand, showed her the whole group—chattering, squirrelly, terrified. Howard, with his fake smile, looked the most insanely scared of all. Howard! Why wasn't he saying anything? Why wasn't he trying to protect her? She didn't want to follow Mary Stern into the woods with Corky Gorsky. But there Howard sat, frozen.

"You and I are the adventurous types," Corky said.

"Are you really the adventurous type? Or do you just think you'd like to be?"

"All I know is that I have to go out and find out

182

what's going on. That's all I know. It runs in the family."

"Like your father?"

"Why are you mentioning my father? I didn't say anything about him!"

"Well, once you mentioned he was famous."

"I said he *wasn't* famous. Was *not*!"

Fern didn't feel like fighting with him, but she was pretty sure that Corky was hiding something. "I think I'll just go on my own."

"That wouldn't be smart. Campers stick together," Corky said.

Hester chimed in. "That's right! You need to have a buddy system."

Maxwell said, "That's right. That's what we always do."

"No, we don't," Marshall said.

"Yes, we do."

"Not always!"

"You can go alone," Corky said. "But I'll just follow right behind you."

"Oh, okay," Fern said. "Fine. Let's go fast. We've already wasted a lot of time."

Corky ran to the screen door, peered into the ring of cabins and slipped out.

Fern started to follow him, but then quickly turned back and looked at Howard. His face was pasty white and nearly blank, but then he looked at her pleadingly.

"Don't go," he whispered. "Fern, don't!"

It was too late. He should have spoken up for her earlier! But no, he'd been too afraid. Hadn't her grandmother and the Bone agreed that they were like brother and sister? Shouldn't Howard have acted like a brother? Fern shrugged at Howard angrily, grabbed her backpack and walked out the door.

She stuck close to the cabin and its shadow. The camp was quiet. Other campers were in their cabins, under strict orders. Fern looked for Corky, but she couldn't find him. He'd already slipped into the woods.

Gus Watershed was setting up a ladder in front of the mess tent. He was clanging noisily, but when Fern ran from one cabin to the next he turned, cocking his head as if he'd heard something. She stopped in a cabin's shadow and held her breath. Then a long black car pulled into the driveway.

Gus Watershed froze for a moment. Then he walked, all tough and stiff legged, toward the car, his white cane leading the way. As usual, he was toting his minicooler. "Gus Watershed," Fern heard him boom. "How can I be of service?"

The car window glided down and someone talked softly but urgently.

"Oh, yes, yes, I gotcha," Watershed went on.

And then the door to Holmquist's deluxe house opened up, and Holmquist himself was holding one end of a stretcher that was being hauled out the door. Holding the other end was an old woman. *Auggie Holmquist?* Fern wondered. *His mother? The one Nurse Hurley thought was a bad egg?* The body on the stretcher was quite still under the white sheet. All Fern could make out was the patient's head wrapped in thick white bandages.

Nurse Hurley came bounding out of her cabin now, charging across the circle to the stretcher. "Why didn't you call on me?" she yelled. "For goodness sake, Holmquist!"

"Don't talk about things that don't concern you!" the old woman shouted back.

"And this concerns you, Auggie?" Nurse Hurley countered. So she was Auggie the bad egg! "You were the owner of a bait and tackle shop. What do you know about someone who needs medical attention?"

A bait and tackle shop! *That's* where Fern had heard the name Auggie before. Auggie's Bait and Tackle. The Bone had been sent to jail for stealing from Auggie's Bait and Tackle, but he'd never even been there. It was an old woman who'd accused him. It was Auggie! Fern felt her cheeks go hot. How could they have sent her father to jail! She was outraged.

Just then a man stepped out of the long black car. He was wearing a beautifully tailored suit with a bright blue striped tie and shiny shoes. "Claussen!" he called out. "How are you, my boy?"

185

The body on the stretcher sat up a little. "Don't," Claussen said. "Tell them not to, tell them to stop—"

"He's been talking nonsense!" Auggie interrupted. "He's seeing things. His thinking isn't at all clear."

"Let him speak!" said Nurse Hurley.

"Who?" Claussen's father asked. "What?"

They were all huddled around him now—Holmquist, Auggie, Watershed, Nurse Hurley and Mr. Peevish. Holmquist was looking around as if he were scared, as

if he were looking out for spies—like Fern in the cabin's shadow. He didn't see her. Watershed's broad chest was blocking his view. Holmquist's eyes went on touring the trees, the edge of the murky pond.

"What is it?" Claussen's father asked, dipping down close to the boy's head.

"Tell them to"—and here he paused, gathering his strength, and then he shouted as loudly as he could— "STOP DRINKING FIZZY!"

Watershed stumbled backward, startled by the outburst.

But Auggie didn't flinch. "He's unwell," she said quickly. "Hurry up now. This stretcher is heavy." She pulled Holmquist on the other end toward the car, but her jerky movements jarred Claussen. The stretcher flipped and the boy tumbled out, landing on his stomach.

"My goodness!" cried Nurse Hurley. "Gus!" she called, looking around for help to lift Claussen. But Watershed had disappeared.

Mr. Peevish called out, "Are you all right? Is he okay?"

Fern saw Claussen, his white body bandaged all over, the white gauzes spotted with blood from his puncture wounds and scratches. His face shot up, a pale, freckled face with no traces of a beak in it. None at all. He was just a regular boy, and he saw Fern there in the cabin's shadow. Though he was far away, he reached out for her. Fern couldn't tell if he was asking for help or trying to reach out to save her. His bandaged hand extended, his pink fingers splayed. But Fern couldn't wait. In the hysteria that followed Claussen's tumble from the stretcher, Fern took her chance to run into the forest.

THE BREATHING TREES

THE FOREST WAS DARK. THE SUN PRESSED DOWN
from above but was blocked by the towering trees'
thick, leafy limbs. At first Fern saw nothing. Her eyes
needed to adjust. Slowly the trees emerged. The ground
was mossy, uneven, pocked with holes and burrows.
Fern was thinking about Fizzy. She was sure that there
was something wrong with it. Maybe it was poisoned in
such a way that it made the counselors so mean?
In such a way that it made them turn into animals at
night? She wasn't sure.

And where was Corky? He'd wanted to stick
together!

Finally Fern could make out two trails. She couldn't

remember which one she'd taken the night before—or if there had been trails at all; it had been so dark. But then a small tree on one of the trails swayed. It seemed to have a hand, and the hand was waving her in. Of course, it couldn't be a hand. It was green and leafy. Still, Fern took it as a sign and headed down that path. She couldn't erase Auggie and Holmquist from her mind. They'd looked relatively normal, but what kind of people were they? They'd sent her father to jail while her mother was pregnant, and her mother had died. The Bone had never gotten to see her again and Fern had never gotten to see her at all. The Miser had wanted to put the Bone away. The Mole had arranged it. Auggie and Holmquist were in on it too. All these pieces were related. But how did they fit together?

Fern trudged along the path. The forest was so dark and so quiet that she wished Corky would show up. She didn't trust him, but she didn't like being alone, either.

"Corky?" she whispered. There was no answer. The path led to the murky pond and to a small, muddy clearing near its shallow edge. She raised her voice. "Corky!" she said as she stepped onto the mudflats.

"I'm right here, Fern," Corky said, but the sun was now reflecting off the pond and it stung her eyes for a moment. She couldn't see anyone.

"Where?" Fern asked, closing her eyes and rubbing them. "Corky?"

"I'm right here," he said again.

But when she opened her eyes, no one was there. Fern was standing alone, looking into the forest. "Corky?" she called again. Staring, she saw the glint of stars in the trees. Low and high, it seemed like the dark trees were filled with them, all in shining pairs. But they weren't stars. They were eyes.

"Corky?" she said. "Are you in there?" She tried to sound casual, but the eyes were narrowing, and she remembered the white bird that had charged her the night before. Everything was silent except for a collective breathing that had just begun—deep breath in, deep breath out. The eyes in the forest were narrowing to intense slits. A pair of eyes moved forward, stepping out into the light.

It was Gus Watershed with his little cooler. He was tall, hulking, swaying a bit as he walked toward Fern, led by his tapping cane.

"Let's stop pretending, Fern." He was shrinking slowly as he spoke. Sharp hairs were rising up from his skin. His eyes grew black and shiny. His minicooler was shrinking too, turning into a sack. Watershed swung it onto his back and it was suddenly a tattered backpack. "This comes as surprise to you, doesn't it, Fern? The blind bus driver. Old useless Watershed. You never

191

thought I'd be capable of anything, did you?" He was now an ugly, hairy body topped with that ugly bloom of a nose, a furry mole with darting eyes and sharp teeth. "Is it a surprise, Fern? Is it?"

Fern didn't answer. She was expecting to have Corky Gorsky turn on her, not Gus Watershed. "Where's Corky?" she asked, her heart pounding loudly in her chest. All around her the breathing got louder, deeper, faster, more angry sounding. It wasn't coming from the Mole. It wasn't coming from the eyes. Fern was searching through the trees to see if she could find Corky, and she noticed that the tree trunks seemed to have rib cages, rising and falling with each breath. The trees themselves were alive. Did they want to attack her too?

The Mole showed his sharp teeth. He said, "Bring him out."

And then Corky appeared, a vulture clamped to each of his shoulders. The vultures' claws had pierced his skin through his shirt, which was spotted with blood. He was pale. He said, "Fern, I tried! I'm not so good at this. It's my first mission!" Mission? Fern was confused. What was Corky apologizing for? She couldn't tell. "You'll have to save yourself!"

She turned one way and then the other, but she was blocked by the glinting eyes, the heavily breathing trees. She turned to the pond and quickly waded in, but Mary Stern rose up, gills flapping. "No," she said, her voice gurgling and pleading. "Don't make this harder."

Badgers, skunks, foxes and squirrels nudged out of the underbrush. The Mole nodded, and two large birds descended from the trees, grabbing hold of Fern's shoulders. Fern and Corky stood in the middle of a growing circle of creatures. The animals with their human eyes, their human lips, closed in tighter. They showed their claws, their teeth.

"It's too bad when an accident happens at camp," the Mole said, sitting on his haunches. "An attack from a wild animal. Just dreadful. And there's only one way to stop it now. I need something. Do you know what I need?"

"No," Fern lied. She knew that the Mole wanted the book so that he could shake out a crown of some sort. "How could I know?"

"You must know, Fern. You must."

"I know you threatened the Miser," Fern said angrily, remembering the Miser's sad face.

"Have you seen him lately? I'd like to have a word with him, too." The Mole's eyes darted around.

"You better not hurt him!"

"Little old me? I'm just a mole. Who would be scared of a mole?" He smiled slowly, revealing his sharp teeth.

"I'm not." She wasn't telling the truth. She was afraid of the Mole.

"Oh, Fern. Oh, Fern, Fern, Fern. So brave! I know

how you once defeated the Miser, but you had the Great Realdo's help, didn't you? And now all you've got is Corky Gorsky."

"Hey, wait a minute," said Corky. "I don't think you realize who you're dealing with! I'm Corky Gorsky, special agent. Here to protect and investigate."

Fern glanced at Corky—skinny, pale, pinned down by the vultures. He didn't look anything like a secret agent. "What? You're a secret agent?"

"Well, this is my first mission. I was supposed to protect you. I was an interrogator, but I got promoted." Momentarily forgetting the circumstances—that he'd been captured and was failing to protect and investigate—Corky broke into a proud little smile.

"You only got promoted because of your daddy!" the Mole remarked coldly. "I'm not the least bit concerned with you, no matter if your father is the head of the agency."

This made sense to Fern. Corky's father *was* famous. He was a very famous secret agent. And Corky was just doing the best that he could. Corky asked questions because he'd been an interrogator. "Did you try to hypnotize Howard to like you?" Fern asked.

"It was just a technique to try to get him to confide in me."

"You shouldn't have. That was tricky! And it didn't work!"

"I'm sorry, Fern. I've made a mess of everything!"

"Well, are you two quite finished?" the Mole interrupted. "You won't be saved this time, Fern," he said, rubbing his paws together, his dirty claws folding over one another. "Why don't we make this quick?"

"Make what quick?" Fern felt her stomach rise with fear.

"Well, I'm doing away with you. You are not in the royal line, dear," the Mole said, taking off his backpack and rooting through it. Fern thought of her own backpack on her back right now and the precious books hidden inside it—especially the one that the Mole was after. "You may think you are. My grandfather and your grandfather may have been friends, but my grandfather had no business handing over my lineage, my royalty!" Fern thought of her grandfather. He had died in the war, when Fern's mother was little. Fern thought of her mother growing up without him. The Mole pulled out a bottle of Diet Lime Fizzy and drank it with what seemed like overwhelming thirst. In fact, he drank and drank and swallowed and swallowed, his eyes closed tight, until the bottle was completely empty. "Especially not to the likes of you! You aren't one of us!"

"I don't know what you're talking about," Fern said. Royalty? She wasn't royalty. She thought of the crown. Was that what he wanted? A royal crown and scepter? Was there a royal line of Anybodies? Was there a ruler— a king or queen?

"Don't pretend with me, Fern! Your little friends may not know who you are and what you're bound for, but I do!"

"I'm not bound for anything. I'm an Anybody, but I'm not royalty."

"You don't know, do you? You really don't know." The Mole blinked at her incredulously.

"Know what?"

"The Great Realdo is your grandmother's royal name. She holds a royal position that must be handed down from one generation to the next. But your grand-mother shouldn't have gotten to be royalty in the first place. My grandfather gave your grandfather *The Art of Being Anybody*, because he said that his grandson was too weak to carry on the royal line. Do I seem weak to you?"

"No," Fern said. Could the Mole jump? Could it leap at her with its sharp teeth? She looked around quickly for a stick, something to protect herself with. She saw a fallen branch not far away, sitting in front of a fat hollowed-out log.

197

"Well, I'm not. And he didn't want to hand the royal line to my sister. Not a girl! Not in that day and age! But then your grandfather died in the war, and that left only your grandmother and your mother, a little girl. She could've become the next in line, taking over for the Great Realdo, but she gave it up because of a matter of the heart! The heart, HA! And the Great Realdo must pass on the royal line soon. Very soon. And you have the book, Fern. There can only be one ruler. Your grandmother may want to live the simple life and let the Anybodies rule themselves, but she's wrong! What is royalty if it doesn't live in a castle! Wear jewels! And occasionally roar, 'Off with your head!' But the castle sits empty and the jewels are in a vault, unworn! And the people whose heads should be off still have them on."

Now the Mole was so close to Fern that he reached out and ran a claw lightly across her neck. "But not for long. My name will soon rule the Anybodies once and for all. The crown and scepter will give me all the power that I need. And those two things, Fern, can be found in only one place in the world, the one place where these things are described with enough accuracy to be shaken out. *The Art of Being Anybody* by my grandfather, Oglethorp Henceforthtowith—of the royal line!"

Fern realized two things: first, that her grandmother could be living a queen's life, but had chosen to run a boardinghouse and live in a quiet world of books, and second, that she was talking to the grandson of the author of the famous, one-of-a-kind book, the very book that was right now in her backpack. "Bort? Bort Henceforthtowith?"

"No, not 'Bort,'" the Mole said angrily. "My name is BORT. And it is spelled *B-O-R-T*—capitals, underline!" The Mole regained his composure. He circled Fern. He sniffed at her backpack. "We both have backpacks, Fern. And we put things that are dear to us inside them." He sniffed at her backpack once more and Fern was sure she'd lost. It was all over. The end. But then he was distracted. "What's that noise?" he said, tossing his flowered nose over his shoulder to have a better look, then rattling his head so a few more clumps of dirt shook loose. He was a filthy mole with dirt stuck in his claws.

Now Fern heard something too. A snapping twig and then someone hollering, "GO! GO! GO!"

Out of the trees came a loud, wild screaming herd—Golgatha, Hester, Maxwell and Marshall, Dolores Laverne and, loudest of all, Howard. He'd come to save her! Fern's heart did a little skip. They were wielding sticks and yelling. Fern was overjoyed to see them, but Howard most of all. And their distraction worked. The vultures pinning Fern and Corky to their spots released them and lifted. But a brawl broke out. The animals seemed rabid, but the campers, including Fern and Corky, were fighting ferociously. They armed themselves with branches. Howard and Golgatha and Hester were beating away vultures. Dolores Laverne was taking on a beaver. Maxwell and Marshall were wrestling vicious racoons. Corky was trying to handle an angry fox. The buzzards kept diving and clawing. Fern saw Dolores Laverne's braids unwind from the top of her head. They rose up in the shapes of two snakes and struck at the birds' claws. When the birds glided over the pond, Mary Stern snapped at them. She was on the campers' side after all! Even the trees were fighting against one another. Some were trying to snatch the campers, locking them in their limbs, but other trees would lash out. It was as if the forest itself were divided. Some wanted to help Fern. Others were clearly on the Mole's side. They beat one another, leaves and sticks and nuts raining down madly.

And the Mole enjoyed the fight. He was small but determined. He lunged at Fern and bit her legs. She tried to get away, but he pounced again. Fern tripped over a hole and fell, and the Mole was in her face, his teeth bared, his mouth foaming. Fern hit him with her stick. But although he was small, he seemed to have the strength of Gus Watershed. Fern couldn't get him to loosen his grip on her throat. She was rasping for breath.

And then she heard a rapid beat of paws growing louder, and barking. The dog—the Seeing Eye dog with the one brown-spotted ear—pounced on the Mole, and they began to roll around on the mudflats in a horrible battle. The Mole was biting the dog again and again. She was bleeding and howling and rolling while the Mole seemed to stab at her with his giant teeth. Fern's heart was racing. She clenched her fists. She felt like crying. She thought of her mother. She could still smell the lilacs on her skin. It seemed in that instant that the whole world had gone crazy—the wings and claws and teeth. Nothing is ever what you expect it will be. Life is always changing, and the dog is being attacked. *That Mole,* Fern thought, *is going to kill her! She is going to bleed to death like my mother.* Life is always turning on you when you least expect it.

Fern felt something inside her melt away and her body began to swell. It grew large. Her backpack ballooned up into massive shoulders. She could feel her teeth lengthening from her gums. Her arms grew bulky and covered in fur. She didn't know what she had become, but she knew that she had transformed into a powerful form. She threw her head back and bellowed. Everyone froze. The birds scattered and the animals charged off into the forest. The dog had gone limp by now. She lay on the mudflats, looking lifeless. The Mole looked up. Fern bellowed again and the Mole dashed away, disappearing into the underbrush.

THE HERMITAGE

FERN COULD TELL BY THE STRICKEN LOOKS ON the other kids' faces that she was some sort of very scary animal. They stood staring at her. Howard was dumbstruck. His jaw dropped. The stick he'd been swinging around fell to the ground. Even the snakes on Dolores Laverne's head were motionless, gawking. Fern didn't have time to reassure them that she was still Fern inside. She was mostly concerned about the dog. Fern felt the weight of her upper body fall forward. She landed on her two front wide, furry paws with thick black claws and scurried to the dog's side.

The dog's eyes drifted open. There was a long, jagged

scratch on the side of her face. The dog spoke. "Are you okay, Fern? Are you okay?"

The dog could speak? How had the dog known her name? She'd gone limp already by the time Fern had transformed. Fern wanted to talk to the dog. She had roared quite successfully, but she didn't know if she was going to be able to speak. She opened her mouth and thought about the words she wanted to say and then said them. "You're hurt. You need help. I know a nurse."

"No," the dog said. "No. I need to go home to my hermitage. I can help myself."

"You're the Hermit that Watershed warned us about?"

She nodded. "I am. Do you hate me like the others?"

"No," Fern said. "Of course not! You saved me."

"Did I?"

"Yes!" Fern said. "You can't walk to your hermitage. I'll carry you there."

Fern turned then and looked at her friends, the good friends who'd come to save her. She just now realized how dirty and bruised and scratched up they all were.

Corky Gorsky stepped forward, his shirt still bloody, his Band-Aid crusted with dirt. "Look, I can take these guys back. We should stick with the mission."

"What mission?"

"Did I say mission? Let's just pretend that nothing has happened. And you, Fern, you should take off. Return when you're no longer a . . . a . . ."

Fern was dying to know what she was exactly.

"Well . . . a grizzly bear, I believe," Corky said.

A grizzly bear! Wow. Fern had truly transformed into something quite astonishing. She was completely surprised and more than a little proud!

"By then I'll have a plan," Corky said.

"Howard," Fern said, "Corky is—"

"A secret agent," Howard said, still a little shaken by the image before him—Fern, a grizzly! "And Gus Watershed is <u>BORT</u> the Mole. I know. We heard it all from where we were hiding."

Golgatha, Hester, Dolores Laverne and the twins all nodded.

"Go to Nurse Hurley," Fern said. "She'll take care of you. And don't drink any Fizzy, no matter what happens!"

"I heard that, too," Corky said.

"So did we! Who yelled it?" Howard said.

"Claussen Peevish before they took him away. It's tainted somehow. I'm not sure. But I think it's what got these counselors under the Mole's control."

"Interesting," Corky said. Then he started walking down the trail back to the camp.

Howard turned to follow him, but then he stopped. "Fern," he said, "you did it! I mean, you really did it! You're, well, you're, you know . . ."

"What do you mean?" Fern asked. She saw his eyes

shining with admiration, but she wanted to *hear* a compliment from Howard.

Howard couldn't do it. He shook his head. "You know, Fern. Don't make me say it!"

Fern was disappointed. She'd hoped he would say it. She watched him as he filed back to camp with the others. Dolores Laverne was the last one. She turned back at the last minute. "Fern," Dolores Laverne said. "Can you imagine?" She pointed to the snakes her braids had become. "I didn't know I could!"

"Neither did I," Fern said, looking down at her large grizzly bear body. "Neither did I!"

The wounded dog directed Fern down a path in the opposite direction. The path wound beside the pond and then across a wide field. It was late afternoon now, and the golden light made everything—the trees, the grass, the clutches of wildflowers—seem like they were wearing bright halos. Fern was walking quickly through the tall, cool grass, because the dog was getting heavier with each step. Or was it that Fern was getting weaker? She looked down at her bulky arms and they had shrunk. Some of the fur was retracting. Other clumps were drifting off her like dandelion quills. Her hunched shoulders turned back into her backpack.

By the time they got to the other side of the clearing, Fern was Fern again—an eleven-year-old girl struggling

to carry a large white dog. Fern was relieved when the
dog told her to stop at a large tree.

"Put me down," the dog said. "We're here."

Fern gently lowered the dog to the ground. The dog

wobbled but then caught her balance. She nosed at the base of the tree near its roots, and a small square gave way. It was a narrow doggie door with hinges at the top of the square. The dog nudged her way through, the door swinging behind her.

Fern bent down. "I can't fit in this little door," she said, pushing it with her hand. She stood up and looked at the tree. Doggie doors are usually found inside of real doors, and so Fern stared until she saw the outline of a human-sized door. Fern looked at the spot where the knob might be and there was a bulbous bit of wood. She put her hand on it and pulled. The door opened.

There was a thin set of circular steps that led down into the ground. Fern walked down them. "Hello?" she said.

At the bottom of the stairs it was very dark. She could make out only a small lit cookstove with a pot of milk already warming on it, and a small bed next to the stove. Despite the little ring of flame and the fact that it was summer, the room was cool and moist as a cave. The walls were mossy and lined with shelves of odds and ends—Chinese checkers, teacups, doilies, and a nice selection of leather-bound books, jars of marbles, buttons, ribbons and bird feathers. Jars of gum balls and licorice and lemon drops. There was also a good number of musical instruments—a French horn, a flute, bongos.

"Do you want something to drink?" the dog said. "I'm warming milk."

Fern turned in the direction of the voice and saw a woman standing there. She was slender and fair. She wore bandages on her arms, and there was a long stretch of gauze taped to her cheek. She wasn't too much taller than Fern, and she was wearing a long white dress.

Fern didn't answer the question. She was still surprised to find herself here. She was looking around the small, cluttered space. Fern could smell the milk on the stove and the mossy earthen walls. "Where's the dog?"

"I'm the dog," the woman said. She lit a small candle and stepped closer to Fern. Now Fern could see that she wasn't very old or very young. She was perhaps Fern's mother's age, if Fern's mother had lived. The woman had the beginnings of kindly wrinkles around her eyes, and curly hair. "I'm the white dog, or I was, but now, I'm me, myself."

"But who are you?"

"Do you want some licorice?" The woman was holding up a jar.

"Yes, please," Fern said. "I'm starving."

209

"Transformation takes a lot of energy. You'll get very sleepy soon as well." She unscrewed the lid on a jar. Fern took out one stalk, not wanting to seem greedy. But the woman nodded, meaning, *Go on. Take more.* Fern smiled and took two more. The woman nodded at the bed, indicating Fern could take a seat, and so she did.

"I'm Phoebe Henceforthtowith," the woman said, moving to the stove, where she poured cups of piping hot milk.

"You're a Henceforthtowith? Like <u>BORT</u>?"

"He's my brother," Phoebe said sadly. "But I don't even know him anymore." Phoebe gave Fern a cup of steaming milk. Fern sipped it. "He blames me because he went almost completely blind as a boy. He had a high fever. My parents and grandparents tried to convince him that things would change. They tried to attune him to the inner workings of the changing world so that he could get better quickly. But he was stubborn. He decided that he was sick and that he'd always be sick. He is nearly blind, you know. I've told him that his blindness can still transform into sight. But he doesn't believe it, and so his blindness is stuck. It's why he can only take the form of a mole or, perhaps, a bat. Bats can't see very well either." She sat down in a small cane chair across from Fern.

"Did you know that Gus Watershed was <u>BORT</u>?"

"Oh, yes. I knew all along. Mickey, the other bus

driver–handyman, didn't show up this summer—oh, he was a sweet, insecure, messy kid, really. And there was Gus Watershed to take his place. Well, I knew it was my brother, and I wondered what he was doing. So I snooped—as I do everywhere; a fly buzzing around the files—and found out that you were going to be on that bus. I wanted to take of care you, make sure you made it to camp safely. I guess I still want to take care of my brother, too, even after all the pain he's caused me." She looked at Fern. "How could he believe it? A stray Seeing Eye dog that can help someone drive shows up just when he needs one? Does that really ever happen?"

Phoebe had been expecting her, had wanted to keep her safe. It was a nice feeling. "But didn't <u>BORT</u> know it was you?"

"<u>BORT</u> doesn't know much of what's going on outside of what's going on with him. He has trouble seeing in more ways than one."

"Why does he blame you for his blindness?" Fern asked, sipping the hot milk.

"I was the last thing that he saw. Me, turning into a songbird to sing him to sleep. But he despised me. He was jealous of how easily I could transform as a little girl. He wasn't as good at it, you see."

"He told me that his sister couldn't be part of the royal line because she's a girl." Fern paused. "I couldn't be part of the royal line. I'm not royalty to begin with."

211

Phoebe looked at Fern. Tears floated in her eyes. She said, "Oh, Fern!" She smiled and then she started laughing. She wiped the tears off her face. "Oh, there's so much to tell you!"

"Does it have to do with Oglethorp Henceforthtowith and *The Art of Being Anybody*? And a certain crown?"

"The art! Ha! He was only scratching the surface, but yes, Oglethorp, my grandfather, was of the royal line. It is a long royal line. It goes back centuries. Oglethorp was the one to pull all the writings together and clarify them with his own sense of order and talents."

"It isn't very clear," Fern said. "No offense."

"No, it's not. But it is all there, under one binding. His son, you see, my father, Alexinsofaras Henceforthtowith, only wanted to sell newfangled gadgets—toaster ovens and washing machines. He had no interest in being an Anybody. And so my grandfather waited for him to have a son. A daughter would be of no use. He thought girls, Fern, can't be great Anybodies." She smiled with her chin held high and her eyes somewhat lowered. It was a cool look which meant that, of course, he was terribly wrong. "My mother had twins. A girl and a boy, but the boy, Bort, was wrongheaded. He was naughty and frightful and a little bit wicked. Once he tried to steal the book from my grandfather. And my grandfather gave the book to my father and sent us to visit a good friend of my father's—your grandfather. You see, your grandfather and my father and Dorathea, your grandmother, were all very good friends at camp, even though my father had no talent. And so when the time came to change the royal line—which can only be transferred in times of dire emergency—my father suggested his good friends who'd married and had a little girl named Eliza and who were planning to have a big family with many children. Surely one would be a boy. Surely."

Here she picked out more licorice, handing some to Fern. "But your grandfather died, Fern, in a war while still young. And your grandmother was left with the book, and she didn't care if her only child was a girl. She didn't care if she wasn't a man. She kept the book and she raised her daughter with it. And now there is you, Fern. You!"

"You're a twin and you came to my grandmother's house when my mother was young," Fern said, remembering the part of her mother's diary that had come clear to Howard once.

"Yes, when my father was dropping off the book. Inside that book is a description of the royal crown and scepter. Whoever wears the crown and holds the scepter is automatically the—the king or, as it is now, queen. That should be you, Fern, as much as anyone else! I saw the way you turned into that grizzly bear! It was an amazing thing!"

213

"But my grandmother isn't a queen! She doesn't rule a kingdom. She was canning peaches this summer!"

"That's her choice. She could have the castle, you know. But she shrugs it off. Who needs a castle when you've got true power? She rules unseen, wisely, gently. She's a benevolent, almost invisible, ruler."

"Well, I couldn't be a ruler. I've never done anything like that transformation before. It was an accident!" Fern said.

"You turned into a grizzly bear your first time? That's even more astonishing. Usually the first transformation is partial. A pig's tail. Or webbed toes . . ."

"Or braids that turn into snakes."

"Yes, things like that. But a full transformation! And a grizzly at that!"

"I don't know how I did it. I don't know if I'd be able to do it again if I tried."

"You'll learn," Phoebe said. "You'll learn. Things are always changing. You have to be in tune with that, the world's flux. You know that Heraclitus was a great Anybody. He was the one who said that you can't step in the same river twice. And Kafka was dating an Anybody when he wrote *Metamorphosis*, of course. It's rumored that some of the best actors are Anybodies—Samuel L. Jackson and Brando, for instance. Why do you think Jack Nicholson wears those dark sunglasses? So if an Anybody winks at him, they can't tell if he's winked back. And haven't you ever thought that Meryl Streep and Glenn Close are actually the same person? Well, maybe so, and then add a few superstars! But who can blame them? You know roles for mature women in Hollywood are so hard to come by!"

Fern tried to take all this in. It was a dizzying history. Phoebe looked at Fern and must have read her confusion. She brought the conversation back to familiar ground. "Your mother was the one who told me that I didn't need the book anyway, that I could become a great Anybody without it."

"She wrote about you in her diary," Fern said.

"She did?" Phoebe blushed.

"Yes. She wanted to help you, but she couldn't."

"No one could. You see, I deserved the book, Fern. I was as good as anyone else at being an Anybody. But I was denied. I was just a little girl. They dismissed me. They ignored me. And my brother was very cruel to me. Anytime I did something that an Anybody could do, he'd tell me that I was crazy, that I was a freak." Phoebe looked down at her hands. Her voice fell to a whisper. "He turned others against me too. Did you see that some of my own trees were on his side during the battle? Those trees are dear friends of mine!" Phoebe looked up at Fern. Her eyes teared again. "He hated me because I could do things he couldn't. But do you know what I did, Fern?"

215

"No," Fern said. "What did you do?"

"I taught myself. And you know what else?"

"What else?" Fern said.

"I've surpassed them all. Fern," she said, excited now, "let me explain! By goodness, I've waited years to explain this to someone!"

"What?" Fern said. "What is it?"

"Oh, this," she said grabbing a velvet pouch. "No, no, this!" she said, pulling out a high-heeled shoe from her closet. "No, no, this!" Finally she grabbed her teapot, very stout and proper looking. She handed it to Fern.

"A teapot?"

"Yes. You see, Fern, my grandfather could take art—a book or painting, someone else's vision of the world—and he could reach inside it and find something real. Well, I took that a bit further. For example . . ." She got up and shook the flute standing up against a wall in the corner. The flute began to play a happy tune. Phoebe rested it on a chair. The tune stopped. "I stretched that idea this way and that. And I realized that there were amazing riches hiding in *ordinary* things. Like me, Fern. I was ordinary, but there were untold riches inside me that no one was seeing." She smiled. "By the sheer will of my imagination, I learned to turn one thing or place or time into another."

"What do you mean?"

"Now Fern, listen carefully. Through the act of

paying close attention, I've learned how to reach into anything—a hat, a jar, a teapot— and find some amazing surprise that has been possible all along, just hidden because no one took the time to investigate it."

"I don't really understand," Fern said.

"Put your ear to the teapot," Phoebe said. "My mother bought this teapot in London. Go ahead."

Fern put her ear to the teapot, the way you would hold up a conch shell to your ear at the beach. She heard a city—traffic and a funny-sounding siren and the voices of some people talking about the rain in funny accents.

"Reach in," Phoebe said. "And when you do, really think of London. Try to envision it."

(Now, I would not have reached in no matter how nice Phoebe was or how much I trusted her. I'm a little gun-shy, having recently reached into a care package to find a nest of scorpions. But Fern had no such fears. . . .) She was thinking hard. She concentrated on Big Ben and that river she couldn't think of the name of and a city scene with double-decker buses. She folded up her hand and fit it into the pot. Once through the top of the pot, her hand was no longer confined to the teapot. She could reach up to her elbow and then the mouth of the pot widened, and Fern could fit her whole head and shoulders into the pot. Once inside, she saw a little tunnel that grew to accommodate her. Fern found that her head had popped out of the top of a certain teapot

sitting in the window of a pristine antique shop on a London side street. It was raining and the people were rushing by the storefront window. An elderly woman carrying an umbrella was walking a little dog wearing a tiny yellow rain slicker. The elderly woman walked up to the window, and there she saw Fern's head sticking out of the teapot. She gasped, and Fern gasped and then slid quickly out of the teapot and back into Phoebe's underground home.

"That's London, dear."

Fern looked at Phoebe, completely astonished. "I saw a dog wearing a rain slicker!"

"That's strange."

"Is it strange even for rainy London?"

"Yes," Phoebe said.

"Was the teapot made in London? Is that important?"

"At first I thought that was the key. But really the imagination is so much more powerful. You can pull an African elephant out of an Italian gondola. You can step into a grocery bag and end up at the National Gallery if you have an exquisite imagination. It's all about how well you pay attention to the details. What I'm saying is it is an artist's job to look closely at something real in the world. They then paint it or write it or dance it or sing it, and in that process it becomes true—a transformation. I can do that through the art of being an Anybody. I can create transformations of most any kind."

Fern was astounded. She was also starting to feel exhausted. Her eyelids were heavy. Her arms were weak. Phoebe was right. The transformation into a grizzly bear had been hard work. Phoebe put the teapot back on the shelf. She lifted off the bandage around her arm. The scratch was pink, but healed. She pulled the gauze off her face. "All better?" she asked Fern.

"Yes!" Fern said. "That's amazing."

"Oh, I know myself well. I've taken care of myself all these years, you know."

"I have a question."

"Yes?"

"Where do you keep China?" Fern asked.

"In the Chinese checkers box."

"And where do you keep Arkansas?"

"I don't," she said.

"Oh," Fern said. "You've been all over the world then, I guess," Fern said. "You've seen everything."

"No, no. I don't actually go anywhere," Phoebe said. "I'm a hermit, Fern. My parents passed on part of this land to me and gave some of it to the camp. A long time ago I may have had a bit of desire to go somewhere, with someone, but that was a long time ago."

"With who?"

"You'll laugh."

"No I won't."

"Joseph Holmquist," she said. "He used to be a wonderful person. Did you know that?"

"Holmquist? The camp director?"

"There were years when his mother was busy spending the money <u>BORT</u> gave her a long time ago, and he was wonderful. I watched him for those years, staying out here. Being with him without being too close. And just last summer, well, I'd actually shown him who I was. We would sometimes walk in the woods or the fields and talk about philosophy." She shook her head. "But that's all changed since his mother and <u>BORT</u> showed up this summer. And it's for the best, I guess. I don't really need people much."

"But <u>BORT</u> needed you and you helped him, and I need you and you're helping me."

"I suppose I still give in every once in a while, but I try not to."

Fern understood this. Howard wasn't really her brother, but she felt like he almost could be, if he could just love Fern enough. And then they'd always have each other.

Phoebe went on, "I wanted my family to know that I was worthwhile, but they never did. I suppose I gave up." She sighed and patted Fern on the shoulder. "But watching you, Fern, it's sparked something inside me."

"Why? What did I do?"

"I watched you stand up for your fellow campers

221

and hold your ground with Mary Stern, for one thing."

"You saw that?"

"As a caterpillar." She smiled. "I've been watching you very closely, Fern. And there's much to learn from you. Somehow you make it seem worthwhile sticking up for people, trying to understand them, listening and making your way in the mess of people and all the time hoping to do some good for people you don't even know."

The Nobodies. Well, it seemed that Phoebe knew everything about her. Fern felt very loved in that moment. They were both silent. Fern was sure she'd been handed a small miracle—someone had been watching over her, like a mother, and had been taking note.

Fern was weary and heavy headed, too. In fact, she found herself to be lying down now, or nearly so. The backpack was making that difficult.

"I don't think it's a good idea for you to carry *The Art of Being Anybody* around in this backpack anymore, do you?" Phoebe asked.

Fern shook her head, almost too tired to speak.

Phoebe slipped it off her shoulders and unzipped it and pulled out the book—leather with gold lettering and a narrow belt. She pulled out Fern's diary and her mother's, too. "How about if we turn these into three white doves?"

"What?" Fern asked.

"This way the books will be birds. They'll follow

you wherever you go, and <u>BORT</u> won't know a thing!"
Phoebe stared at the books. They began to rattle and
quiver. They grew soft. The books opened and began
to lift up into the air, beating their pages and covers
like wings, until they were wings and the wings were
attached to three beautiful white birds.

"Amazing!" Fern said, her head on a pillow.

Phoebe pulled a
blanket on top of her.

While Fern watched
the birds circle the
room, she thought
about Phoebe as a sad
little girl. It was awful
that she had so many
places to go but couldn't

bring herself to go anywhere. She was
thinking about Phoebe's mean brother, <u>BORT</u>, and how
she had grown into a giant bear. She was thinking about
her mother and the messages in the bottles. She needed
to tell Phoebe about that. Phoebe would help, wouldn't
she? And she was thinking about Mickey, the bus
driver–handyman who'd never showed up. Wasn't he the
one, then, who'd also been the handyman who'd written
such terrible signs . . . never leaving enough room for all
the letters? And didn't that way of writing and that name
match one of the messages that were still in Fern's

pockets? Was Mickey with the Nobodies in a basement somewhere? Fern had so many things she wanted to say, but her eyes were closing. She only had energy for one more question, and this is the one she chose: "Time," Fern said. "You said you could go to any place or any time. Where do you keep the past, Phoebe?" she asked.

Phoebe looked at the three birds, perched on the bed's footboard, preening themselves. She smiled sadly. "Oh, I keep my childhood scattered among the jars, but the saddest parts of it I keep here." And she showed Fern a square pocket sewn on to her white dress right over her heart.

THE SEARCH PARTY

AT THIS POINT, YOU CAN IMAGINE THAT FERN wasn't the only one who was tired out. I'm quite over-whelmed myself. I've had ghastly incidents with an ele-vator, a manhole, a waterfall. I've been attacked by a boa constrictor, scorpions and a flambé dessert! Just this week, I was accidentally mistaken for a rodeo clown. (How insulting! I thought I was dressed rather spiffily!) I'm weary. My nose is running. In addition to this stut-ter, I've developed a facial twitch. I'm bug-eyed with exhaustion.

Fern was embattled, but was dreaming of a nice camp. Her dream camp was filled with buttercups and pollywogs and monarch butterflies and chameleons! A camp without watery macaroni and cheese, shower spiders, marching songs, handbook memorization, a trigger-happy skunk, mean counselors who spent their nights transformed into animals ordered around by a viciously evil mole! Fern walked into Nurse Hurley's cabin. Nurse Hurley was rummaging through her books, slamming each one shut in disgust. "I must save her! I must, I must! She's too young to leave this earth!"

Fern ran into the small bedroom and found a little bear lying there on a cot—a big-eyed little bear. Sometimes in dreams you know things. You don't know how you know them. You just do. And Fern knew that the little bear was her mother.

"Don't forget them!" the little bear said.

And Fern knew that her mother the little bear was talking about the Nobodies. Fern hadn't forgotten them. They weighed on her mind. "But how can I help?" Fern asked. The room grew darker. Thunder boomed in the distance. A storm was coming.

"Life is always changing," the bear said, pointing out the window into the circle, where there were skeins of pollywogs. They sprouted into plump frogs that inflated into horses with thick manes and black hooves. At the next round of thunder, they darted quickly away. "People get stuck. Don't let them."

Nurse Hurley was in the room. Her cheeks flushed, she was breathless with grief. "I can't save her," she told Fern gravely. "I can't."

But the little bear who was Fern's mother told Nurse Hurley it was okay. "It's all going to work out."

Now Fern could hear the Nobodies calling her name. Mickey was there too, calling and calling. And her mother said, "Go, Fern. Go!"

Fern woke up, breathless, but the thunder continued and her name was still echoing overhead. It wasn't thunder after all. It was someone banging on the tree, or more than one person. And it wasn't her mother and Mickey and the Nobodies. No, this was an angry chorus, chanting her name.

Phoebe was a dog again. She was padding around nervously. The doves were nervous too, flitting around the room. "It's still dark," Phoebe said. "You must go, but I'll be watching over you. I promise. I'll find you when you need me."

"Really?" Fern asked.

"Yes," she said. "It's amazing what Anybodies can do when they're needed."

"I'm needed," Fern said. "BORT has locked the Nobodies away in a factory basement somewhere. Do you know anything about that?"

"BORT's Fizzy Factory?"

"Of course! Yes, yes, I guess that's right. <u>BORT</u> owns Fizzy. That makes sense. That's where they get all their bottles! Do you know where it is?"

"I don't know where the factory is. But you don't need to know. If you don't find it, Fern, remember that you can create it!" Phoebe lost her dog form. She stood up into herself. She hugged Fern.

And then Fern climbed the stairs inside the tree. At first she peeked through the doggie door. A pair of big work boots blocked her view, but she could tell from all the noise it was a large gang. It was dark out there, but light coming from above, an orange glow, cast dark shadows.

Then she heard someone yell, "Down there! She's down there!"

The boots stepped back and Fern saw the worn knees of a pair of jeans and then the full ruddy face of Gus Watershed himself. Fern was looking right into his brutish face, his eyes hidden behind the pair of sunglasses he always wore. "Is it her?" he bellowed right in her face.

"It's her all right!" someone shouted from behind him.

"Listen to me and listen good," he said. "You, Fern, are being kicked out of camp altogether, once and for all. Holmquist has ordered it. I'm taking you to Holmquist's office." He lowered his voice. "And then I will drive you home—you and me alone on my bus! So why don't you come out now?"

A bus ride alone with Gus Watershed, the Mole, BORT? She was certain she'd never survive it. But she didn't have a lot of options, either. Fern stood up. Her palms were sweaty. How was she ever going to get out of all this? How could she save the Nobodies? It didn't seem possible.

"It's okay," Phoebe was urging from downstairs. "It will work out. The only way out is through."

Fern opened the door and stepped out of the tree. Her mother's diary, her diary, and *The Art of Being Anybody*, disguised as the white doves, rose up from behind, flew up into the air and perched on a tree limb.

Fern was encircled by counselors in their nearly human form and campers. But where were Howard and Corky? Golgatha, Hester, Dolores Laverne and the twins? It was hard to make out faces. The skunk counselor was holding a torch, but the shadows were distorting. Fern could see Mary Stern hiding behind the badger-faced counselor. Would she help Fern now? Was she still under the influence of Fizzy?

"Kicked out! Kicked out!" a chant began. "Kicked out! Kicked out!" It gained momentum. Mary Stern was mumbling along in unison. Gus Watershed grabbed Fern by the arm and started marching her forward.

"Where's Howard?" Fern shouted above the chanting. "And Corky Gorsky?"

"They're in Holmquist's office. They're witnesses to all the rules you've broken, and they're accomplices!"

"Why am I getting kicked out of camp?" Fern asked.

"You ran off! And you were staying with . . . with . . . with . . ."

"Phoebe?" Fern said.

"The Hermit!" Gus Watershed spat. "We warned you!"

"But she's nice! She's good! If only you'd ever given her a chance . . ."

"You don't know what you're talking about!"

Watershed charged ahead, taking great strides with his white cane banging across the field before him. Fern had trouble keeping up, and so Watershed yanked her along. The gang kept chanting, but underneath the loud chorus, Fern could hear a few small voices of dissent.

"You can't kick her out," the small, wavering voices called out. "You can't!" The small voices created their own chant to combat the louder one. "You can't kick her out! You can't kick her out!" Pretty soon the gang stopped chanting so they could hear the other, smaller voices more clearly. Finally, by the time they reached the murky pond and the trail through the woods, all that was left was the small chanting of the wavering voices.

"You can't kick her out! You can't—"

"What's this!" Gus Watershed yelled, turning on the group at his heels. "Of course we can! She's broken the rules! Be quiet!"

Now, in the brighter light of the glowing torch, Fern recognized a few faces peering out of the crowd. Maxwell and Marshall smiled and waved. Golgatha and Hester looked tough. Dolores Laverne was there too, her braids back to braids again, not hissing at all.

"The handbook clearly states," Golgatha said in a clear voice, "that running away isn't punishable by expulsion."

Hester went on, "To be expelled, you have to have wronged another camper."

"Fern hasn't hurt anyone!" Maxwell cried out.

"That's right!" Marshall said.

"Fern has been heroic!" Dolores Laverne went on.

All of their memorization of the handbook paid off after all. Howard would be proud. He was such a proponent of knowing the rules.

This outburst took Watershed by surprise. "What? The handbook? Have you been reading the handbook? Who gave these campers their handbooks?"

Mary Stern didn't say a word. She slipped back into the crowd.

"It's all there in black and white," said Hester.

"Well . . . well . . . well . . . but . . . but . . . ," Watershed stuttered for a few minutes. The crowd of campers and counselors shuffled their feet. They were nervous. Had Watershed led them astray? Were they kicking out some innocent camper? Watershed could feel the tide change in the crowd.

One of the campers asked, "Has she done anything else?"

And another questioned, "Has she done anything really wrong?"

"Shut up!" Watershed cried. "And be happy that everyone is allowed Fizzy Drinks now! Just drink the bubbles and enjoy!"

Fern hadn't noticed the bottles before, but now she could see that it wasn't just the counselors. All the kids were also drinking Fizzy—except, that is, her friends.

Fern's friends beamed at her triumphantly. But then Watershed turned to Fern. "Not so fast! Who says she hasn't injured one of the campers?"

"I haven't," Fern said.

"You haven't?"

"No!"

"Well, am I the only one who heard Fern screaming Claussen Peevish's name on the night he was attacked?

Maybe it's just my keen sense of hearing, but I distinctly made out one clear voice that night, and that voice was the cold, evil voice of Fern, calling the name of her victim while she attacked him!"

"That's not right!" Fern said. "You've got it wrong!"

"Did anyone else hear her?"

"YES, YES!" the counselors shouted.

"But that's not it—," Fern said.

"Did you or did you not scream Claussen Peevish's name the night he was attacked?"

"I did, but . . . but . . ."

"Enough!" Gus Watershed's mouth stretched into an evil grin. "Claussen Peevish. Sweet Claussen Peevish! What, oh what, did you do to him?" He turned to Hester, Dolores Laverne and Golgatha. "Mary Stern, lock these girls up!"

HOLMQUIST AND HIS MOMMY

EVEN THOUGH THE SUN WAS BEGINNING TO RISE,
the bonfire was lit, and it looked menacing. Fern
was afraid of the campers all hopped-up on their
Fizzy. They had strange glints in their eyes—like they
wouldn't mind pushing Fern into the bonfire itself. She
felt like crying, but she was too angry to cry in front of
everyone and so she bit her lip. As Watershed dragged
her toward Holmquist's office, someone was poking a
sharp stick into her back, hissing, "This is for what
you did to Claussen. Poor Claussen!"

"I didn't do anything to Claussen," Fern kept
saying. "Watershed knows what happened to Claussen.

234

Watershed's to blame! He's the Mole! Gus Watershed is the Mole!"

But the counselors' jeering drowned Fern out.

"Don't bother telling them!" Gus Watershed countered, and then he leaned down and whispered in Fern's ear. "No one is going to listen to you, Fern! You're evil, remember?"

The stick digging into her back, her head ringing with angry kids, Fern was scared. Who would listen to her? How would she ever get out of this? She looked up

into the sky to see if the white doves were following her, but it was too dark.

By the time they arrived at Holmquist's house, the kids had begun chanting, "Evil! Evil! Evil!"

Watershed swung Fern around so they were face-to-face under the porch light. "Now you're in for it, Fern!"

Fern couldn't hold it in any longer. She started to cry, because she was thinking back on what she'd wanted out of camp in the first place and how she'd gotten this nightmare instead.

"Stop crying," Watershed said. "Stop it!"

Watershed folded up his long cane and poked the doorbell with it. There was a loud chime. The crowd quieted down. The door opened. It was Auggie. Fern recognized her from the scene around Claussen's stretcher. She had a pruney face and a sour, puckered expression.

"Here she is," Watershed said, shoving Fern toward her.

"Come on in," she said to Fern.

"Tell Holmquist that Watershed delivered her," Watershed said.

Auggie glared at Fern. "I'll tell him, sir," she said.

"Good," he said, and then shut the door.

"Sit here," Auggie ordered.

Fern sat down in an overstuffed wing chair in the entryway. She sat lightly, though, just on its edge.

"I'll be right back." Auggie shuffled down the hall.

Fern didn't like Auggie. She knew that Auggie had helped to put her father in jail, and as she sat there she imagined what it must have been like for her father to be in jail for stealing from a bait and tackle shop that he'd never even been to! Now that she, too, had been unjustly accused— in her case, of hurting Claussen Peevish—she had a better idea of how her father might have felt.

It was very quiet in the house except for the constant hum of the air conditioner. It seemed soundproof, actually. All the curtains were drawn. In fact, in this entranceway sitting on an overstuffed wing chair, Fern had no real feeling at all that outside the door and down the walk was a noisy, sweaty, stinky camp of wild, chanting, angry children who hated her. In here, there was a whiff of pipe smoke, mothballs. There was a grandfather clock, ticking. And there were lamps, making the furniture glow warmly. All of it made Fern angry. The enemy was living so comfortably!

When Auggie reappeared, waving Fern down the hall, Fern had to remind herself that she was in trouble. What she really wanted was to confront Auggie and Holmquist and make them confess. She thought of Howard and Corky. She wondered how they were doing. Were they being interrogated? Were they being dragged around and accused and poked with sticks?

The old woman opened a door with a brass knob. Fern stepped inside the room. It was lush with beautiful Persian carpets and a large oak desk with a gold blotter and an ivory-handled letter opener.

"Come in," Holmquist said calmly. It was still early in the morning, and Holmquist was wearing a silk robe. His hair was rumpled and his eyes were baggy.

Howard and Corky were sitting on the sofa. They swiveled around to see Fern. Howard had donut powder on his cheeks. He looked ridiculously pleased. His pockets were stuffed with candies, and there was a scroll of Candy Buttons in his lap, picked nearly clean. All this irked Fern. She'd been dragged through the woods by a wild, hateful gang carrying torches, and here Howard was happy as a milk-fat cat. Corky looked pensive and nervous.

Holmquist motioned to the sofa and Fern sat down between the two boys. Howard smiled a white-powdered smile and handed Fern the box of donuts. "Here," he said. "Have some!"

Fern scowled at him, and he looked a little sheepish. Fern wanted to prove the point that this was not a time for donuts! But sometimes folks are just too hungry to prove a point. Fern was a tough kid, but she wasn't Gandhi, for goodness sake. So she started in on a donut herself.

Corky whispered urgently, "I can't believe I've been captured on my first mission! It's very embarrassing! My father's going to have a fit!"

Howard glanced at him. "We're not captured!" he said, "We're eating donuts! And, for once, we're in a normal house, not one of those stinky cabins! This is an improvement."

Fern looked at Holmquist, but he was looking at Auggie. "Please shut the door on your way out," he told her.

"I'll stay and listen," Auggie said. "Thank you kindly!"

"I asked you to please leave. I need some privacy to

talk to the campers."

"And I said I was staying. So you can put that in your pipe and smoke it!"

"You know I really don't like it when you show a blatant disregard for my authority," Holmquist said, adding, "I prefer a subtle disregard."

"It's unbecoming. These little fits and snits of yours. Unbecoming!" And suddenly Auggie put on a very sad, pouty face. "You're going to make me cry!"

"Don't, don't cry, Mother. You can stay."

"I don't want to be where I'm not wanted." Auggie started for the door.

"No, stay! Please stay!" Holmquist begged.

"Are you sure you want me?"

"Of course I do!"

"Well, in that case . . ." And so Auggie sat down, but she was still huffy.

Holmquist smiled at Fern. "Do you want anything? Anything at all?"

"No, thank you," Fern said. "I just want to say that I didn't hurt Claussen Peevish! I never laid a finger on him! He was coming to my rescue when—"

"I'm aware of the situation," Holmquist said.

"Oh, but Mr. Watershed said that I was going to get kicked out."

"We can discuss that later."

Auggie didn't like that. "No, no, discuss it now! We

had that meeting today! You have to—"

"I know what I have to do! I've lived my whole life knowing what I have to do!" Holmquist said. He turned back to Fern. "How was the hermitage? Did you meet the Hermit?"

"Yes."

Holmquist leaned forward. He looked suddenly boyish and sincere. "How is she?"

"Um. Fine."

"Oh, stop asking about that silly woman! You and that woman!" Auggie interrupted. "She's no good for you. Not my boy! I've told you that one million times!"

For the first time he ignored his mother. "Did she mention me? Did she say anything about me?"

"She said that you used to be a wonderful person. That's it."

"Don't listen!" Auggie screeched at her son. "She's no good!"

Fern was really peeved now. "She *is* good!"

Holmquist smiled at Fern, and he looked very kind. "She said that?" The news seemed to make him happy and sad at the same time.

"Yes," Fern said.

Holmquist went all dreamy eyed, and Auggie took over. She stood up and paced before the three of them. "We need to make sure that crazy woman isn't allowed near the campers!"

"Why would you do that?" Fern asked. "You couldn't!"

"One day," Auggie said greedily, "we'll put the Hermit in a place better suited to tending to her needs. She needs a fine institution for people as crazy as she is."

"That's not the deal I made!" Holmquist flared up. "I made it clear that I'd go along as long as she's not touched!"

"My dear son. My pride and joy," Auggie said softly. She opened a small minifridge and pulled out a bottle of Fizzy. "You haven't had your breakfast. You're cranky. Have a drink!"

"No, thank you," he said. "I have my own." He nodded to an opened bottle of Fizzy on his desk, and then he glanced at Fern, raising one eyebrow, which Fern took as some kind of attempt to communicate with her. What was he trying to say, though? Fern knew this, however: Holmquist still loved Phoebe, and his role in all of this mess was designed to protect her. But Fern wasn't completely ready to forgive him.

Auggie turned to the kids on the sofa. "The Hermit's brother is very concerned about her too, you see. He only wants what's best for her."

"Her brother? The owner of the Fizzy Corporation?" Fern asked.

"You know him? Fine fellow. Fine, fine, fellow," Auggie said. "And you, my dears, all three of you, have not been pleasing him or me or my son. Not any of us. You've caused too many problems and, well, you've committed crimes against this camp! So you must be dealt with!"

They weren't safe, and neither was Phoebe. Auggie was standing by the window talking about the powerful qualities of <u>BORT</u> and her son, about wealth and power, things she seemed very fond of. Holmquist was sipping his Fizzy, but when Fern looked at it closely, she noticed that it had no fizz. No bubbles lining its sides. It wasn't a Fizzy Drink at all. Fern needed to get out of here and to take Corky and Howard with her.

Howard was much too happy with the donuts and candy to be helpful. And Corky was just shaking his head, probably thinking about disappointing his famous father. It was up to Fern. She looked around the room. She felt trapped, but she remembered what Phoebe had taught her—London in a teapot, and what amazing things an Anybody can do when they really need to! *I can create help!* While Auggie was still yammering, Fern slipped one of her hands behind her back and started digging around behind the sofa cushion.

"<u>BORT</u> is a strong leader, not one to be messed with. We were of service to <u>BORT</u> some time back, and it paid off. I've made a good bit of money, in my day. And he"—she turned to Holmquist—"he just wanted to live here in peace. Well, peace is expensive too! It can't be funded forever. You've got to be kind to the hand that feeds you! When <u>BORT</u> needs us, we're here for him! <u>BORT</u> always repays a kindness. And a son must always do what his mother says. Isn't that right? Aren't you happy in your beautiful new house—not some teepee in a field? Aren't you happy in your silk robe?"

Holmquist scratched at the tag of his silk robe. Auggie went on and on, giving a grand speech about how it pays to give <u>BORT</u> what he wants, but Fern was thinking of people who could help her—Dorathea, the Bone and Phoebe. Fern shoved the donut box onto Howard's lap and he dug in to polish off the last one. She was thinking and digging and thinking of how silly Howard had been when he'd wanted help, shaking a hunter from a book to kill a rhino. Fern would get real help. Good solid help. Suddenly Fern felt a hard rim. She pulled. It was metal in the shape of a circle, no, in the shape of a funnel. She pulled and pulled. She even grunted, which got Holmquist's attention. And then she pulled so hard that she stood right up and turned around and used both hands. And it wasn't a funnel. No, it was the wide-mouthed barrel of a gun. Good Old Bixie's gun. And do you know who was attached to it, pouring out of the sofa cushions, falling onto the ground, in an ungainly heap, all sprawled out onto the floor? Good Old Bixie himself. Fern wanted to protest. She hadn't meant to pull out Good Old Bixie, but he had crossed her mind! He was dazed, but keen eyed. He was a hunter, after all. He jumped up, wielding his gun.

"What?" Auggie said. "What in the devil?"

"Point the gun at her," Fern said, "and . . . and, keep an eye on him. . . ." Fern pointed to Holmquist, but he looked pretty happy that Fern had turned the tables. He may have even looked relieved.

"Get together there, you two," Good Old Bixie said.

And so Holmquist and his mother stood side by side behind the oak desk with their hands in the air.

"And what about him?" Good Old Bixie asked, nodding at Corky.

"Corky's fine," Fern said. "And you remember Howard, Good Old Bixie."

"Oh, Howard, of course. Righto."

There was a quiet moment when everyone just kind of took in the new turn of events.

Fern said, "I know what you two did. You set up an innocent man, my father, the Bone! And he had to go to jail, and he never saw his wife again. That was surely an evil thing to do."

Auggie didn't look one bit sorry. "We did what we had to do to get ahead!" she said.

But Holmquist looked very contrite. He said, "It's weighed on me, you know. I tried to change my life, but she's always dragged me back. Always," he said, glancing at his mother. "Remember, I used to be a wonderful person, right? Is that what she said? Tell Phoebe I was asking about her, if you see her! Tell her that I'm watching out for her . . . from a distance."

"You can't do a very good job of loving someone from a distance. You two have to figure that out!" Fern said.

Holmquist looked at her wide eyed. He nodded. "You're right, Fern."

Auggie elbowed him in the ribs, but he didn't seem to notice. Howard put the empty box of donuts on the oak desk, smiled politely and gave a belch, and the four of them—Corky, Howard, Fern and Good Old Bixie— eased out of the room and then ran down the hall and out the front door.

PART 5

THE FACTORY BASEMENT

BASEMENTS, BASEMENTS EVERYWHERE

IT WAS MORNING. THE CAMP HAD QUIETED DOWN.
No one was in view except for six faces peering out the
window of Girls' Cabin A—Marshall and Maxwell,
Golgatha, Hester, Dolores Laverne and Mary Stern.
Good Old Bixie, Howard and Corky headed toward
the edge of the forest. But Fern ran to them as fast as
she could. They were staring at her in astonishment.
Corky was waving his hands and mouthing, *No! No!*
But Fern didn't see him and she had to do what she
had to do.

Fern knew that she needed to devise a way to get
to the basement of the Fizzy Factory, where she might

find the Nobodies who needed her, but she wanted to talk to Mary Stern first. Fern stopped in front of the window.

"I'm sorry about everything," Mary Stern said quickly.

"It's okay," Fern said. "Watch out for these guys." Fern nodded to Marshall, Maxwell, Golgatha, Hester and Dolores Laverne.

"Be careful, Fern!" said Dolores Laverne.

Fern nodded and ran back to the forest's edge.

Corky was panicked. "Where to, Fern?" he asked.

Good Old Bixie was gazing into the trees, looking, Fern expected, for big game. He was, after all, a big-game hunter, and he still didn't know what he was doing here. He was muttering to himself. "Important to get a feel for the new terrain," he said.

"Which way?" said Howard, with the agitation of a sugar buzz.

Fern looked into the forest. "I don't know."

"I don't either," said Corky. "I should have stayed home! I'm a terrible secret agent! I've already been captured twice!"

Good Old Bixie was testing the wind with a licked finger. "Not sure which way," he said. He scratched his head and gazed off into the distance. He gave an exhausted sigh. "Blast it, men!" he said in a loud, angry voice. "Why don't we just ask that good fellow there if he knows where the big game is hiding in this wilderness? We're in some kind of primitive civilization. We should talk to the natives!"

At this moment, walking out of his cabin, was none other than Gus Watershed. His head snapped around. "Who is it? Who's there?" He teetered forward. "Talk to me!"

"Run!" cried Fern. Howard and Corky took off. Fern grabbed Good Old Bixie, who was in the middle of saying that he thought he recognized this chap from a bull roast in Morocco.

"ALARUM! ALARUM!" Watershed shouted. "ALARUM! COME QUICK!"

Just at that moment Fern saw three white doves flapping above one of the trails ahead. And so Fern decided to trust the books—disguised as birds—and follow them. Zipping along the trail, Fern could hear the swarm of children and counselors pouring out of their cabins.

"Get them!" Watershed was screaming. "They're dangerous!"

Fern, Corky, Howard and Bixie had a good lead, but the kids were fast. It was hard terrain, what with the mole holes to jump over and around. Fern sprinted out in front. "I've got an idea," she said.

She was thinking about what Phoebe had told her about stepping into other worlds. A grocery bag could transport you to the National Gallery, wasn't that right? Where could she find something to climb into? Fern zigged and zagged, dipping under low branches. The four of them were approaching the place where Fern had encountered the Mole the night before. She tried to remember the spot. Soon she spotted the fat hollowed-out log.

"Here," Fern said, "follow me!" The birds stopped and flitted back to Fern. She said, "Think of basements! Basements!" And she climbed in first. Howard was next, and Good Old Bixie and Corky after him. The three birds landed and walked in, heads bobbing, after everyone else.

The log began to widen. Fern was scared and tired. She longed for the comforts of home, but she kept inching forward. Finally she could hear a distant gurgling noise. Soon her hands and knees were wet and she was plodding through a few inches of water. The hollow log also opened upward. There was a beamed ceiling with some exposed pipes. Fern stood up. The first thing she noticed was the stacks of books, the second thing was the overwhelming presence of peach preserves. This was her grandmother's basement!

She looked at Howard and Good Old Bixie. They were all still breathless. "This isn't the right place!" Fern said.

"Where are we?" Corky asked, a little dazed. "This is very unusual!"

There was a drain in the middle of the floor, but it was slow. The basement was still flooded. There were the flowerpots that the Miser never did get to bring upstairs.

"Oh, I know where we are!" Howard said, relieved. "I'm tired and I feel a little sick. I think I may have eaten too much. I'm going to go upstairs. I need to take a nap."

Good Old Bixie grabbed Howard by the arm. There was a gleam in his eye. He was enjoying himself. "A nap? That's for the weak of heart! What we need is a plan. And a bit of luck. What say our chance of finding a herd around in the wilds above ground? Or at least my rhino. I miss my rhino, you know. Good fellow, that rhino!"

"Look," Fern said. "What we're in need of is a basement. Not just any basement. We need the basement of the Fizzy Factory. The Nobodies need us."

This wasn't enough information for Corky. "Who are the Nobodies? What's this about?"

"I'm not sure who they are, but they're trapped by BORT and he needs to be stopped."

"The agency has been watching BORT for years, but they've had no luck pinning anything on him."

"BORT and Auggie have some sort of deal, and they want to do away with me," Fern explained. "And they want to send Phoebe to some institution. You heard them!"

"Who's Phoebe again?" Howard asked.

"The Hermit. And she's wonderful. She's brilliant and wonderful! So are you all going to help?"

"I'm in," said Corky. "Though I've been sort of useless!"

"I'd like your help," Fern said.

"Okay then! I'll try!"

She turned to Bixie. "No herd hunting. Can you do that?"

"Say no more!" said Bixie. "Comrades in distress! I can help!"

"And you?" Fern said to Howard, last of all.

"I don't know. You know this isn't my thing, Fern. I'd rather go upstairs and curl up with my math books. You don't really need me." And then he glanced up. "Do you?"

Fern didn't want to say that she needed Howard, but she needed all the help she could get. And she really did want Howard there, even if he'd be no help whatsoever. "I do need you," she said. "I do."

Howard gave a small smile. "Well, I didn't know you were desperate! Okay then. Okay, I'm in."

Fern found the next basement by jumping into the biggest flowerpot over and over until the bottom expanded. (In the past few months, I've become afraid to walk on almost any surface. How many times have floorboards come loose right under my feet? As of today, twenty-two.) There was then a short drop. It was a bakery cellar that Howard recognized from an odd job the Bone had had years ago as a pastry chef.

The next was the Drudgers' renovated basement, which never ever leaks. It's dry and tidy. Not one spider. Not one stinky-basement stink. Not one toad in a window well. Nothing. The three birds didn't even fly around in it—it was too pristine for birds.

"What's with the birds?" Howard asked.

"Friends of mine," Fern said.

The next basement was a root cellar that Good Old Bixie recognized from a story that he thought he'd made up to entertain himself while out hunting his rhinoceros. It was an Australian root cellar, packed with strung-up hams and empty jugs. The story was about an escapade in the Outback, where he had been nearly paw-kicked to death by an angry mother kangaroo. Perhaps it was true after all. Good Old Bixie was no longer a dictionary version of a big-game hunter. He was a real person who had to have real memories, right?

Fern got to the next basement through a gunnysack. She was blinded by shining gold and silver—awards, plaques, medallions of honor and service. She didn't know where she could be. The walls were covered with photographs of a man with bristly hair, shaking hands with what appeared to be dignitaries, important people with stiff hair and formal smiles and crisp suits.

Bixie popped out next. "My, my!" he said.

Next came Howard, who said, "What is all this?"

Corky was last. When he stepped out of the gunny-sack, all he had to say was, "Oh. I thought this might happen."

"Where are we?" Fern asked him. The birds stood on the tops of award statues.

"My parents' basement. My father keeps his agency awards here. He's, well, he's highly honored." Corky pointed to the pictures lining the walls—smile after smile after smile.

"Geez!" Howard exclaimed. "And he's your father?"

"Hey, is that so hard to believe?" Corky said defensively, but then he sagged. "I guess it is. I sure have bungled this! I'm going to have to go back to being in charge of polishing his statues after this!" He pointed to a golden statue of a man saluting. "That's how I scratched my nose," he said. "That little statue's elbow. I bumped into it."

Fern paced around the overpacked basement. Wrong basement after wrong basement was beginning to take its toll on her. She felt like she was going to cry. She hung her head. "I don't know what I'm doing," she said. "I want to help, but I don't know how." She sat down on the floor, tears welling up in her eyes.

"I know how you feel," said Corky.

"Me too," said Bixie.

"Ditto," said Howard.

Something about the way that Howard said, "Ditto," something about his little frustrated sigh, reminded Fern that Howard had felt this way about the Drudgers that night he was trying to decode Fern's mother's diary. And that was when Fern's mother's diary had come clear to him for a short time. Fern was thinking about this when an idea struck. What if her mother's diary was hypnotized to be of use to those in need? What if it only revealed what it needed to reveal to help the person who was reading it at that very moment?

Fern said, "Maybe that's it!"

"That's what?" said Howard.

Howard and Bixie and Corky looked at one another and back at Fern, but Fern was already cooing at the birds. "Here birdie, birdie, birdie!"

"We don't have time for this bird play now!" said Bixie.

"Fern? What is it?" Corky asked.

"I need my mother's diary."

"But why are you calling the birds?" Howard asked.

257

"One of them is my mother's diary!"

One of the birds dipped closer to Fern. "Are you my mother's diary?" she asked the bird.

The bird winked. Fern winked back. She opened her hands and the bird dipped down, landing in her palms. It spread its wings, and the wings became the open cover of the book. Its feathers ruffled into pages.

"Wow!" said Corky. Howard and Bixie stood there, staring in amazement.

"Thank you!" Fern said, and then she gently started going through her mother's diary. It was a mess, page one, two, three, four . . . Nothing made any sense. It was the same old gobbledegook. But then somewhere around page thirty-two, Fern saw a word she recognized and another and another. Fern gasped. Her eyes started galloping across the page. She read aloud:

Phoebe and I were playing in the lake at Derson's farm today. Bort was there, on the shore, but he doesn't know how to swim. He never did, even before he was blinded by that fever. He said, 'I'm going frog hunting.' And Phoebe said, 'I collected rocks this morning, and I can make them into frogs if you want pets, Bort.'

Bort said he didn't want pets. He said he didn't need her frogs and she couldn't turn rocks into frogs anyway.

"'Come in and swim,' I said again, because it would be more fun for Bort to swim than to collect frogs when he can't see the frogs.

"'We can help you learn how,' Phoebe said. 'We can help you so you're not afraid of water.'

"But then Bort turned on Phoebe. He started shouting from the shore, hopping mad. 'I'm not afraid of anything and I don't need your help. How many times do I have to tell you that? You're nothing! You're worthless!'

"'Be quiet, Bort!' I said. 'Just be quiet.' But it was too late. Phoebe was already sinking underwater, and I watched her twist into the shape of a golden sea turtle and slip away. It was the most beautiful thing I've ever seen, but sad, too, because it was almost like she couldn't help it. She lets her heart go and her mind follows and then her body.

"Bort walked off with his cane, and I went to shore. I collected our things. In Phoebe's bag, the rocks had already turned into frogs. I let them go and they all hopped away."

Yes, Fern was right. Her mother had hypnotized her diary to be unreadable except when someone needed something in it, really and truly. And did this passage help Fern? Yes, it did. It taught her two things.

One: <u>BORT</u> had been afraid of water and probably

still was. Fern remembered that <u>BORT</u>, as the Mole, couldn't swim. He'd been paddling that little bucket boat in Fern's grandmother's basement.

And, more importantly, two: if you let your heart go first, your mind and body will follow.

Fern had to seek out the Nobodies with her heart. The first time she looked for a basement, she'd been thinking of home. As for the bakery basement: had Howard been dreaming of sweets again? And the Drudgers' basement—had Fern been thinking back fondly to simpler times? Or had Howard? And the Australian root cellar—had Good Old Bixie been fixed on the idea of adventure? And Corky Gorsky? Had he been thinking about his father and the grand collection of trophies?

She looked at her *compadres*—Bixie, Corky and Howard. She said, "We have to feel for the Nobodies in our hearts. Deep in our hearts. The only way to find them is to love them, to truly want to save them."

"That's not what they teach secret agents to do," Corky said.

"I don't love the Nobodies," Howard said. "I don't even know them!"

"I'm a big-game hunter," said Bixie. "I'm not about to be going all soft!"

"Okay," Fern said. "Who do you love? Start there, at least."

"Well, I don't love you. That's for sure," Howard said to Fern. "Even if you are like a sister, you sure are the difficult kind of sister! How did you get me into this mess, anyway! I was eating donuts and then you came along and I was being chased by a gang of crazed campers who wanted to tear me to pieces!"

Howard was pretty angry but, actually, this little speech made Fern smile, because she knew at that moment that Howard *did* love her as a sister. He'd just called her a sister for the first time, and they were both only children, so this kind of thing meant a lot. In fact, Fern felt a warmth spread through her chest. It was a tenderness she hadn't expected in herself. *Howard loves me,* Fern thought. *He really does.*

Okay, one down, she said to herself. She turned to Bixie. "What about you?"

Bixie was even easier on the subject of love. His cheeks bobbed a few times and he wiped his nose. "Well, I guess I could be honest with you." He paused and took a deep breath. "I don't really want to kill the rhino."

"You don't?" Howard asked.

"Honestly, no. I've gained a lot of respect for that beast. I've come to admire the beautiful creature. Once I saw him grazing in an open field. I could have shot him easily enough, but I didn't. I just watched him, and, well, I don't know what I'd do without him, you know?"

"Huh," Fern said, a little surprised by Bixie's confession. "I guess there are all kinds of love." And she looked at Howard for a second, just glanced at him. Howard loved her and well, she had to admit she loved him a little too. If Bixie and the rhino could be pals, well then, Howard and Fern could be too.

Good Old Bixie took out a large white handkerchief and blew his bulbous nose.

Fern smiled, and then turned to Corky Gorsky. "And you?"

"Well, the fact is that I want to impress my father because I love him."

"Okay, now what we have to do is to think about this love. I will think about the Nobodies and you three think of what you love. I will follow my heart, and you follow me."

Fern closed the book, closed her eyes and held the book in her hands while thinking of the bird, its heartbeat, its beak and feathers. The book grew warm and soft, and when she opened her eyes it lifted up from her hands and became a bird again.

She unloaded a few trophies out of a wicker basket and crawled in. The wicker pricked Fern's knees and the palms of her hands as she made her way through. Fern was sweaty and anxious. The Nobodies needed her. She felt an ache of desperation.

"Ouch!" Howard was muttering behind her. "Ouch! Ouch!"

"Blasted wicker!" said Bixie. "And my jodhpurs keep creeping up!"

Finally Fern felt cold cement flooring. She could hear the chug of machinery. She could smell smoke, something burning. She stood up slowly. Her eyes were met by nearly a dozen pairs of eyes shining through the dusty light. She smiled. "We're here!"

THE NOBODIES

THE BASEMENT WAS DARK, DIRTY AND FILLED with boxes and newspapers, empty Fizzy bottles and objects of art. The Diet Lime Fizzy factory overhead grumbled so loudly that everything in the basement seemed to be trembling with the vibrations. The birds circled up high and landed on rafters, where they jiggled. There was the stench of something burning, and the high, small basement windows were open but provided almost no breeze. Fern could barely see the Nobodies at first. But she heard them.

"Is it her?"

"Is it really her?"

"Do you think?"

"It is!" the tallest, oldest boy said. "I know it! I told you so!"

The whispers scuttled up and down and then, as Fern's eyes adjusted to the murkiness, she saw them.

The Nobodies were all children, except one who was in his late teens. They were staring at Fern from where they stood on either side of a very long table filled with candelabras and doubloons, statues and paintings, jewels and gems. The Nobodies had been packing the items in boxes, balling up newspapers as filler so that the items were protected. Now they started to wander away from the yawning boxes and approached Fern slowly. Their clothes were tattered and dirty. They looked hungry and sad and hopeful all at the same time.

"Fern?" one asked. It was a little boy about Fern's age.

"Yes," Fern said. "It's me!"

"She's come to save us!" The kids started cheering in low, hushed voices.

"This is Howard and Corky and Good Old Bixie," Fern said. "And who are you?"

"I'm Oliver," the boy said. "And this is Heidi and Huck. This is Pip and James and Anne."

The tallest boy introduced himself. "I'm Mickey."

"Mickey!" Fern said. "Did you work at the camp?"

265

"Yes," Mickey said. "But then I got taken away in the middle of the night and landed here."

"By <u>BORT</u>?"

"Yep," Mickey said. "I knew you'd come!" He beamed.

Fern looked at the Nobodies. She looked into their faces, and in each one she found something familiar. And then it dawned on her who they were. "I know you. I know all of you from books," Fern said. And there was something else. Something that they had in common, but she couldn't put her finger on it. "You're all . . . Well, you have one thing in common. . . . You're all . . ."

"Orphans," Oliver said.

"That's right," Fern said. "It's so nice to meet you all. It's such an honor."

Bixie took off his pith helmet and bowed a little. Howard and Corky waved shyly.

"Why are you all here?" Fern asked.

Right at that moment a voice came booming from a loudspeaker that was mounted on the ceiling. A sharp, needling voice began to sing:

"I'm a little despot short and stout.
Here are my sharp teeth. Here is my snout.
When I get all steamed up, hear me shout.
Just tip me over and pour me out!"

"It's him," the orphans said to Fern. "It's <u>BORT</u>."

"I ain't afraid of him," Huck said, but Fern could tell he was afraid.

Then there was a metal clang from the ceiling and a loud buzzing noise. A circle overhead began to lower, and suddenly there was a round-bottomed metal cage lowering itself down, down. Inside the cage was the Mole, turning circles and snapping his teeth.

The Nobodies shrank back. As the cage touched down, a door flipped open and the Mole walked out and sat up on his haunches.

"So you found me, Fern. You found my little family here, tucked away underground."

"This isn't your family," Fern said.

"They're perfectly happy with me. They're orphans, poor things. Oh, but orphans work so hard! They don't know much about family anyway. They don't know any better than being happy here, working for me! Isn't that right?" He sneered at the Nobodies and snapped his teeth. They didn't say anything. Oliver, who seemed to be in charge, looked at Fern hopefully. But Fern still wasn't sure what her plan was.

Good Old Bixie had his fluted gun trained on the Mole. "Tell me when to shoot," he said to Fern. "Just give the word."

The Mole eyed Good Old Bixie in a steely fashion.

"Not yet," Fern said. "First I want to know some-

thing. What is all this? What are you doing?"

"Oh, this," the Mole said, waving his hands around admiringly at all his loot. "Well, Fizzy is just a cover. I make my real money by shaking items out of books and selling them. Why not shake a workforce out of the books too? And what better workforce than little orphans? I'm quite rich, you know." And with that he clapped his hands and suddenly a cloud of bats slipped out of vents on the wall and swarmed Bixie, who dropped his gun and tried to cover his head. Howard let out a screech and grabbed hold of Fern's arm. The bats chased Bixie into a corner of the basement, where he sank to the ground and balled up. At that moment a mass of spiders poured out of the vents too, and they scurried over Bixie, hundreds of them, trailing their strands of web until he was securely pinned to the wall. Then they webbed his gun to the ground. When they were done, the spiders crawled back to

the vents and the bats, too, dispersed and slipped away into the ducts.

"What's this?" Bixie said, his voice muffled by the webbing. "You can't do this! I demand civility!"

"Oh, civility! I miss it sometimes, but not very often." The Mole then turned to Fern. "I think we should finally take care of this once and for all. You, Fern, must go. It's the only way, my dear, to restore the proper order. Which is, of course, to have a Henceforthtowith in charge. That's what is needed, a reestablishment of the royal line."

"But what's that burning smell?" Fern asked, stalling.

"Oh, that. It's books, of course. Who needs books once you've shaken them dry?"

Fern felt a little sick. Heidi covered her mouth. She'd started to cry. Anne wiped her nose on her dirty sleeve and clung to Huck, who jutted out his jaw trying to look brave.

Howard was still holding on to Fern's arm. But now he'd started to pinch at it. It kind of hurt, and it was terribly annoying as Fern was in the process of possibly facing her own death. And Corky was coughing, a weird, dry, fake cough. She glared at both of them, but they just stared back at her with big eyes that quickly shot to the wall behind the Mole.

As the Mole carried on about the royal line, occasionally snapping his sharp teeth, Fern saw a shirt appear right from the side of the wall. The shirt unfolded and landed lightly on the basement floor. It was followed by a slip and two skirts and a few cardigan sweaters. That's why Howard had started pinching her and Corky had been coughing. Fern glanced at the Nobodies, who were clumped together, all of them with their eyes glued to what was going on behind the Mole. Bixie's one visible eye was fixed on the falling clothes too. There was a nice little heap of them by this point, and now, suddenly, there was a shoe. A woman's brown lace-up shoe. A very plain shoe, and it was on a foot that was attached to a leg.

"The Henceforthtowith name. . . ," the Mole was going on. "Our grand lineage . . ."

And then there was another shoe and another leg and the hem of a dress, a little bunched and wrinkled, and a backside that poked out of the wall. The legs were now dangling and the body was half in and half out. Two elbows with rolled-up sleeves appeared. There was a final shove, and then with a huff and a clatter, Phoebe jumped out of the wall and landed squarely, feet first, on the basement floor.

SPRINGING A LEAK

PHOEBE LOOKED AT HER BROTHER. SHE LOOKED at the Nobodies clustered together, frightened. She looked at Good Old Bixie caught in the thick web, and then at Corky, Howard and Fern.

"Let me consider this situation." She rubbed her chin and paused. "This is a very bad situation, and I believe it's your fault." She stared at her brother. "Isn't it?"

"What are you doing here?" he barked.

"I was just digging through my winter trunk, looking for a certain pair of socks. How do you suppose I wound up here?" She looked at Fern. And then she turned back to the Mole. "Why don't we talk, brother and sister, two real people," she said. "Show yourself.

Why not? Show yourself, Bort."

Suddenly all the Nobodies and Mickey reared. "Back away!" Huck shouted out. "There's going to be a fight!" They knew that this woman had made a terrible mistake. She'd called <u>BORT</u> Bort. And they knew what was coming.

The angry Mole rose up, his fur standing on end. He let out a long low hiss. "My name is not Bort. It is <u>BORT</u>! <u>BORT</u>!" He rushed at his sister. He took a leap, his teeth snapping furiously.

"No!" Fern said. "Don't!" She rushed toward them, but there was little she could do. The Mole was tearing at Phoebe's skirts, biting her legs. Little patches of blood dotted her skin. He was lunging and she was retreating, spinning, trying to get him off of her. He grew, snarling and snapping. His fur puffed up; his back grew broad. Fern was wondering what he might become. But he didn't transform. He just became a larger mole, his paws thrashing the air.

Fern yelled, "No! Stop!" She tried to think of becoming a bear. How had she done it? She held her breath and squeezed her eyes shut.

"Do something," Corky yelled to her.

"Turn into a bear!" Howard shouted.

The giant Mole now had Phoebe in his massive grip.

"Save yourself!" Fern yelled, knowing that Phoebe had the power to defeat him. But Phoebe wasn't using her

273

powers. She was remaining Phoebe. And this only seemed to make <u>BORT</u> angrier. Fern grabbed a candelabra and started pounding on the Mole's meaty back. Howard and the Nobodies started to look for weapons too. But there wasn't really time to attack.

When <u>BORT</u> turned to lash out at Fern, Phoebe got free. But not for long. <u>BORT</u> took his great claw and reached for her. He reached right for her heart. Phoebe swayed backward and <u>BORT</u>'s claw grabbed the pocket on the front of Phoebe's dress. The pocket ripped open and then, quite astonishingly, a flood of water poured from that pocket. The flood was so strong that it forced Phoebe up against the wall, where she stood back and watched the great river gush from her. She was the only one who was not surprised.

<u>BORT</u> began to shrink. He started screaming. "I can't swim! Make her stop!"

The orphans started to shout and scream too. Mickey grabbed a few of the younger orphans, holding them up above the fierce tide.

Good Old Bixie was sputtering, "Help me! Help!" And Howard and Corky started ripping the webs down as fast as they could, but the strands were thick and it was hard work. Pip and James helped too.

Phoebe, however, was calm. She looked at Fern with great sadness. And Fern knew that this was the sadness of her childhood pouring from Phoebe, these were all the wrongs that had welled up inside her for years and years.

The flooding went on, and the river from the ripped pocket wasn't letting up.

<u>BORT</u> had shrunk to his regular mole size again. He was pattering around in the water, screaming, "Save me!" The water had already run across the floor and was now rising.

"Show yourself!" Phoebe said to her brother. "Show yourself to me!"

But <u>BORT</u> refused. "Never! I am who you see!"

"No, you aren't. I need to see the real you. I need to see what you've grown into after all these years!"

By now the water had risen up past knee level. Bixie was loose, up and wading as well as possible in his jodhpurs. Howard and Corky were bobbing near James and Pip. <u>BORT</u> was trying to get back to his elevator, but there was a rushing current in the water and it kept tossing him aside.

Fern was thinking ahead. "Get to the elevator," she told the Nobodies, some of whom couldn't swim. "Go! Go!"

"No," Heidi said. "We won't leave you behind, Fern."

"We'll go and get help," Mickey told her. "Fern knows what she's doing."

"Yes," Fern said, "that's right. Go!"

There wasn't enough room in the elevator for Howard, Corky and Bixie—and they wouldn't have left Fern now anyway. They helped the Nobodies and Mickey jam in. Fern flipped a switch, sending them up, up, up to the ceiling, where they would end up on the first floor of the Fizzy Factory.

"Thank you!" some yelled out to Fern. "Thank you!"

But Fern didn't have time to even say *you're welcome*, because the water was rising faster than ever. The Mole was swirling around, gasping, choking. The water was up to Fern's waist. The Mole was sputtering, dipping under the water, scrabbling back to the surface. Soon enough the water had tipped Fern up off the floor. It was over her head now. Fern was swimming to the Mole. The birds were squawking and flapping overhead. "Here!" she said to <u>BORT</u>. "Grab my hand."

Howard and Corky were underwater, trying to pull the emergency exit door open.

"Pull! Pull!" Bixie was shouting from above, but it was no use. The door was locked, sealed shut.

Phoebe was still gushing, but treading, too, in the river she was creating. She was calling out to her brother, swimming toward him. But he was still clawing. Fern was trying to grab him. Even though he was shouting, "Save me!" he didn't want to be touched.

Phoebe said, "Bort, turn into a fish! Swim!"

"I can't swim!" the Mole was yelling. "I'm just a boy. I never learned how. I can't. I'm too afraid! I'm just a boy still."

And then he *was* just a boy. His body grew pink, hair-less and lanky. His snout and whiskers dissolved and his face appeared. Suddenly he was a boy with freckles and wide, terrified, still blind eyes. He was someone Fern had never seen before, but Phoebe knew him.

"Bort," she said. "My brother." She held out her hand and he reached for it, the water from her chest still pour-ing forth, but less so. He turned toward the sound of her voice. "Why?" he asked.

Why what? Fern wanted to know.

Phoebe didn't answer. She simply pulled him safely into her arms.

ON THE AVENUE OF THE AMERICAS

JUST THEN A FACE APPEARED IN A HIGH BASE-
ment window. It was Holmquist. "Phoebe!" he yelled
out. "Phoebe, I'm here. I'm here to help!"

Phoebe, holding her brother in her arms, looked up at
him. The water was raising all of them up. Fern was
surprised to see Holmquist. Then she figured that he'd
decided not to love Phoebe from a distance anymore.

"Joseph," Phoebe said. "You're here."

"Yes," he said, holding out his hand to her through
the open window.

Bort, as a boy now, was still flailing a good bit. The
water was so salty, though, that he didn't even need to

tread. They were all buoyant.

Suddenly the windows were filled with faces. Mickey and the Nobodies. "Here!" they yelled in their various accents. "You can make it out these windows!"

Anne and Heidi were working to pull them open even wider. Huck and Pip and Mickey were reaching in, ready to help haul everyone out. The windows were small, but just big enough. Huck grabbed hold of Fern's wrist and pulled her up. Pip and James grabbed Howard, and next came Bixie, then Corky. Phoebe pushed her brother out ahead of her with Joseph's help. Bort scrambled out the window and collapsed on the sidewalk, soaking wet. Phoebe followed and knelt next to his small shape. She held his hands, Holmquist sitting beside her.

Fern, Corky, Howard, Bixie, Mickey and all the orphans stood back and allowed them a quiet moment.

Bort's blue eyes flitted open. "Phoebe," he said.

"Bort," she said, "you never grew up. Why didn't you ever grow up?"

"I couldn't. I don't know why. I just couldn't." But even as he said this, he seemed to become larger. His face lengthened. He said, "Phoebe, why did you save me? You should have let me drown."

"I couldn't do that."

"But I hated you," he said, growing still broader and longer. "I've always made you as miserable as possible.

I've been plotting to have you locked up for good."

"You're my brother, Bort, and I've always loved you."

"I'm sorry, Phoebe," he said. And he swelled into the shape of a full-grown man, with gentle eyes and ruddy cheeks.

By now, this being New York City, after all, a small crowd had started to form around Fern and Howard, Corky and Bixie, Mickey and the Nobodies.

"What's happening?" people asked.

"What's going on?" asked a pink-haired woman. Her face shimmered with piercings.

"Is this part of a movie?" asked a man with a brief-case. "Where's the crew?"

Fern told them. "They're brother and sister and they haven't spoken to each other in years. He thought he hated her, but now he knows that he loves her, deep down."

"But why are they wet?" a kid with a skateboard asked.

"She kept her sad childhood in her heart, but it burst, like a dam, and it poured out."

"Oh," said the crowd, and they hushed.

And then one woman, an old woman, said, "I had a brother once. I loved him, but he's gone now. And I never said good-bye."

Fern looked up at the old woman, who'd started to cry. She'd started not only to cry from her eyes, but

also, it seemed, from her heart. Her blouse was damp.

"That's so heavy," the boy with the skateboard said. As he started to ride off, Fern noticed that his T-shirt was sticking to his chest.

The man sat down on the curb, wedging his briefcase between his knees, and the water poured freely from him as he cried.

The woman with the pierced face sat next to him, teary eyed. "I have two sisters and a brother," she said.

"I should be nicer to them. What about you?"

"Last time I saw my brother I told him he was no good," the man cried.

The orphans began to gush small floods. Corky and Bixie started to cry too. They were embarrassed by it but couldn't hide it. The force of the emotion was too strong, and so they just had to give in. Howard turned away, but it was clear that he was moved, his own full chest starting to leak.

Fern thought of her mother, and how much she missed her, and how she loved her although she'd never met her. The birds landed at Fern's feet and stared up at her lovingly. One of the birds winked at her, and Fern knew that it was the one disguised as her mother's diary. She winked back and picked up the white bird, cradling it. Fern's heart felt taut and constricted. The bird felt a little wet in her hands, and Fern lifted it up to the crook of her neck. Her heart was leaking too, making a small flood at her feet.

Howard walked up and put his arm around her. "Me too," he said, looking at the creek slipping from his shirt.

And then they looked at each other, really looked at each other for the first time in a long time. "It's not too late," Fern said. She wasn't talking about the books. She was talking about the two of them being brother and sister. And Howard understood and smiled.

One person told the next about the brother and sister reunited and the mystery of the flood of her past overflowing. And as the news spread, others joined in. They couldn't stop themselves. And soon the Avenue of the Americas where Fern and Howard and Bixie and Corky and Phoebe and Bort and Mickey and the Nobodies had just found safety was flooded with the childhoods of the good people of New York. In fact, my dear editor was walking to her office that day when she heard the news and recalled her sister and a deep love and how she missed her. And my dear editor, too, was caught up in the gushing.

The whole crew was swimming again. Even though they were all gracefully lifted up in the salty water, Bort still held tightly to Phoebe. They were rising, able now to look into people's office windows. Secretaries' heads snapped up from their computers, shocked and amazed.

"We've got to do something!" Howard said.

"Do we?" Phoebe asked.

Fern looked at Phoebe. "Can't you do something?"

"I am doing something," Phoebe said. "Sometimes it's more important to be yourself, to be true to that, than anything else. You can do something, though, if you want. You have great abilities."

And so Fern thought. *Well, a river is something that you can reach into,* she figured. Maybe if she reached in, something good would come out. And so she put her hand under the water and let it swirl around until she found the edge of something. She pulled, and then this edge started to nose upward.

"I've got something!" she shouted.

"What?" asked Howard.

"What is it?" Corky and Bixie chimed.

"I don't know, but it's big!"

It was lifting all of them now, lifting them up as if they were all sitting on the edge of a giant steam shovel, lifting them straight out of the water and into the air.

"Hello there!" a voice called out. It was the Bone.

Dorathea was there too. "Hello! Hello!"

And the Bone was at the wheel of his peach-pit boat. Dorathea helped them to the deck, one by one—Phoebe, Bort, orphans and all. "Are you okay?" she asked. "Is all well?"

"This flood!" Fern said. "What can we do about it?"

"It isn't a flood," Phoebe said. "It's a washing, really. Everyone will be okay. In fact, they'll be better. They'll be set free."

Everyone was quiet. They were sailing down the Avenue of the Americas, the wind in their hair, the buildings slipping past, the people bobbing happily, calling out to them. The river was already on the move, subsiding here and there as it poured its way downtown.

The Bone said, "I wish the Miser could see this! I wish his boat could be up here with mine."

Fern wished it too. In fact, there was a collective wish that billowed up from all the people there—even the orphans, who didn't know the Miser; even Bort, who had threatened the Miser, who was still listless from nearly drowning, from all the love of his sister. And Bort meant it. He wanted to see the Miser, happy, in his boat.

And so Fern reached overboard and, as she did, she caught sight of Corky, who looked happy but still sad, too. Underneath Fern's wish to see the Miser, she had a second wish, and before she could unwish—because she wasn't sure how this second wish would turn out in the end (Who does? Who, for example, would have expected this ending?)—Fern let her hand land on an object. She felt the thick edge of something very large. And they all watched the Miser's matching peach-pit boat cut through the surface of the salty river. The Miser was there, wet and bewildered but extremely happy, at the helm. He looked hale and strong again. His adventures on his own in the world far away from Dorathea's house, where he'd once thought he might hide for the rest of his life, must have been good ones. He looked like the captain of his ship, and, well, he was.

He had a passenger, a man with a bristly, short haircut, a sopping version of the man Fern had seen smiling and shaking hands with dignitaries in Corky's basement. He stood up on the deck and staggered a bit, calling out, "Corky! Corky! Where are you?"

Corky shouted, "Here I am!"

And his father spotted him on the deck of the boat where Fern stood. Corky's father took a giant leap from one deck to the next. He grabbed his son up in his arms and said, "I'm sorry. It was too soon. Are you okay? All I want is for you to be okay!"

Corky wrapped his arms around his father. "I'm fine," he said. "I'm okay."

The Miser waved to the Bone, and the Bone waved back—both of them standing proudly at their helms. And, by the Miser's side, like a sturdy, well-fed second mate, was the rhino—his large white horn glistening in the sun.

AND . . . WAIT! THERE'S MORE!

I AM ALIVE AND WELL, FOR THE MOMENT, BUT I'm still writing as quickly and carefully as I can. You need to know that the peach-pit boats followed the out-pourings downtown. They then pulled off onto a side street and got wedged between two buildings. The water flowed on without them, leaving the boats dry-docked in an awkward spot—between a nail salon and, on the other side of the street, the Wok Shop. This caused much confusion, especially because of the rhino. The Bone, the Miser and Dorathea stayed behind to talk to the author-ities. And Good Old Bixie stuck by the rhino's side, determined to make sure he was kept safe.

Bort, Phoebe, Holmquist and Mickey all went back to camp together. They would have to confront Auggie, who would be very confused by the new allegiances, but she'd be forced to concede. Bort needed to rest in the care of Nurse Hurley. Mickey needed to take over his old job again. And Phoebe and Holmquist had to gaze lovingly at each other, and that takes a lot of time.

Along with the three birds, Fern and Howard and Corky and Bixie were told to take the Nobodies with them on the subway so that they could make their way to a train in Hoboken and then home to

Dorathea's house by way of a cab.

The subway ride is of great importance, of course, because it's where Fern and I met. Howard and the orphans were asleep when the subway broke down and they stayed asleep. (Later we'd find out that some flooding of the tracks had caused the delay.)

Fern told me the whole story. And then she sighed. "But the orphans," she said. "Now they don't have books to go back into. The books they came from were burned. We can't shake them back into other books. There can't be two Heidis in a copy of *Heidi*. It would confuse everything. What will we do with them? They'll want to find a home of their own."

"I know what to do," I said. "I know exactly what to do." I was a writer, after all, or nearly so. And although I was maybe the worst writer of all time, one who could single-handedly cause the demise of literature—my writing teacher knew my name! Had announced it to the class! I was still buzzing with pride! "I'll write them into my books!" I said.

And so that's how all of this began. I promised, and I've kept my promise. They are all now in my book, this book, the one you're reading at this very moment. What will become of me? I don't know. Will anyone ever catch my writing teacher? I don't know. But I will go on, making my way in the world, knowing that I've done my part, and I've done it the best that I can.

I suppose there is one more thing.

After I told Fern that I would write the orphans a home in my books, I looked out the dark window and saw a bit of my own reflection—silly, rumpled me, smiling. But the smile didn't last too long. My brow tightened up. I was puzzling over something. I crossed my leg and jiggled my foot. Something about the story was still bugging me. I turned back to Fern. I said, "Well, I've got to know something. Are you royalty or not?"

"Of course I'm not royalty," she said, almost laughing.

"But the Mole said that the crown and scepter are in *The Art of Being Anybody*, and if you shake them out then you are automatically part of the royal line. Did you try that?"

"No," Fern said, suddenly very humble.

"On what page are the crown and scepter described? You don't have to shake them out. I'd just be curious, you know, what the darn things look like. I'd like to at least hear you read the descriptions. Not that it isn't a good story without the crown and scepter, it's just that you left me hanging a little bit."

"Oh, sorry," Fern said, and so she cooed to the fattest bird, which, she figured, was the fattest book, *The Art of Being Anybody*. The bird nestled in her lap, spread its wings and fluffed into the big book with the gold lettering. Fern looked up "crown and scepter" in the index in the back of the book. She mumbled, "Page two forty-two. Two forty-two." She fluttered through and then opened the book to that page.

Sometimes you don't have to shake a book. Sometimes the book wants to give you something so badly that it simply bursts from the pages. The crown and scepter wanted to give themselves to Fern in just this way! When the book opened to page 242, the scepter rose up like a stalk of corn and the crown bloomed like the giant head of a golden flower.

Fern was royalty. We both sat there, flushed and dazed—stunned, really. And then, because we were so nervous about the whole thing, so overwhelmed, we started giggling and then laughing, and then we laughed so hard that we started crying.